DEAD GRAVE

A DEADWATER STORY

OTHER LIVING DEAD PRESS BOOKS

DEAD OF SPACE: BOOKS 1&2, PLAYING GOD: A ZOMBIE NOVEL
KNIGHT SYNDROME: TEMPLARS OF THE UNDEAD
TWISTED FISH: AN AQUATIC ANTHOLOGY
DEAD THINGS (W/AN EXCLUSIVE DEADWATER STORY)
NIGHT OF THE WOLF: A WEREWOLF ANTHOLOGY
JUST BEFORE NIGHT: A ZOMBIE ANTHOLOGY
THE BOOK OF HORROR
THE TURNING: A ZOMBIE NOVEL
THE WAR AGAINST THEM: A ZOMBIE NOVEL
CHILDREN OF THE VOID, DARK PLACES
BLOOD RAGE & DEAD RAGE (BOOK 1& 2 OF THE RAGE VIRUS SERIES)
DEAD MOURNING: A ZOMBIE HORROR STORY
BOOK OF THE DEAD: A ZOMBIE ANTHOLOGY VOLUMES 1-5
LOVE IS DEAD: A ZOMBIE ANTHOLOGY
ETERNAL NIGHT: A VAMPIRE ANTHOLOGY
END OF DAYS: AN APOCALYPTIC ANTHOLOGY VOLUMES 1-4
THE ZOMBIE IN THE BASEMENT (FOR ALL AGES)
THE LAZARUS CULTURE: A ZOMBIE NOVEL
DEAD WORLDS: UNDEAD STORIES VOLUMES 1-7
FAMILY OF THE DEAD, REVOLUTION OF THE DEAD
KINGDOM OF THE DEAD, DEAD HISTORY
THE MONSTER UNDER THE BED, DEAD HOUSE
DEAD TALES: SHORT STORIES TO DIE FOR
ROAD KILL: A ZOMBIE TALE, DEADFREEZE, DEADFALL
SOUL EATER, THE DARK, RISE OF THE DEAD
DEAD END: A ZOMBIE NOVEL, VISIONS OF THE DEAD
THE CHRONICLES OF JACK PRIMUS
INSIDE THE PERIMETER: SCAVENGERS OF THE DEAD

THE DEADWATER SERIES

DEADWATER, DEADWATER: Expanded Edition
DEADRAIN,
DEADCITY
DEADWAVE
DEAD HARVEST
DEAD UNION
DEAD VALLEY
DEAD TOWN
DEAD GRAVE
DEAD SALVATION
DEAD ARMY (coming soon)

COMING SOON

CHILDREN OF THE DEAD: A ZOMBIE ANTHOLOGY
BOOK OF CANNIBALS VOLUME 2
CHRISTMAS IS DEAD: A ZOMBIE ANTHOLOGY VOLUME 2

AUTHOR'S NOTE

This story takes place after book 7 (Dead Valley) in the
Deadwater series

DEAD GRAVE

DEAD GRAVE

A DEADWATER STORY

ANTHONY GIANGREGORIO

WHAT HAS COME BEFORE

Two year ago, a deadly bacterial outbreak escaped a lab to infect the lower atmosphere across America, unleashing an undead plague on the world.

With rain clouds now filled with a killer virus, to venture outside in the rain was tantamount to suicide.

To get caught in the rain and exposed to the bacteria would be an instant death. But that wasn't the end. Once dead, the host body would rise again, becoming an undead ghoul, wanting nothing more than to feed on the flesh of the living.

The United States was torn asunder, civilization collapsing like a house of cards in weeks.

But mankind survived, eking out a dreary existence, always keeping one eye on the sky for the next rainstorm.

Only two years after the zombie apocalypse, the world has become a very different place from what it once was. Gone are cell phones, the internet, restaurants and shopping malls; now all lost relics of a culture slowly fading into history.

In this new world, the dead walk and a man follows the rules of the gun, where the strong are always right and the weak are usually dead. Major cities are nothing but blackened husks, nothing but giant tombs filled with walking corpses. Across America, though, smaller towns have become small municipalities with makeshift walls protecting them from both living and dead attackers. Strangers are not welcome and are either shot on sight or made to move on, that is, if they are not exploited by the rulers of the towns.

Through the destruction of what once was walks a man, crushing death beneath his steel-tipped boots. Before, he was an ordinary man, living a quiet life with a wife and a career, but the rules have changed and so to, has he adapted, becoming a warrior of death who wields a gun with an iron hand, but shows mercy and wisdom when it is needed.

His name is Henry Watson, and with his fellow companions, Mary, Jimmy, Cindy, Sue and Raven by his side, he travels across a blighted landscape searching for someplace where the undead haven't corrupted everything they touch; where he can lay his head down in safety.

Though life is fleeting, each breath means the possibility of one more day of life, and a better future for all.

DEAD GRAVE

The ghouls were everywhere, and Henry Watson raised his Glock and shot another zombie in the head.

The 9mm round struck the zombie in the right eye and blew out the back of its head in a glorious spray of blood and bone matter. But for every one he shot, there were five more to take its place.

"Jesus Christ, Henry, where the fuck did they all come from!" Jimmy Cooper yelled by his side as he let loose with a barrage from his twelve-gauge shotgun.

Only a few feet in front of him, bodies disintegrated into red mists filled with viscera that fell to the ground, to then become crushed by the approaching dead.

"We can't keep this up forever!" Mary Roberts yelled from behind Henry.

"No shit, we need to find a way to break free from these bastards or it's all over!" Cindy Jansen replied.

"Get off, get away!" Sue Anders shrieked as she shoved a decayed body away from her. No sooner did the ghoul fall away then it was coming back at her, but then its head was practically severed from its shoulders by a dark vision with long black hair and fingernails honed to a razor's edge. As the ghoul fell away, clutching at its exposed throat, Sue let out a sigh of relief and said, "Thanks, Raven, that was a close one."

The dark-haired teenage girl nodded. "Just stay close to Henry," Raven said and then was dancing into the ghouls once more. She moved fast, a blur amongst the slow undead, and each time her nails connected with decayed skin, a slice of flesh was missing from the ghouls. She knew how to use her natural weapons well and each time she dove in, an eye was plucked from its socket.

More ghouls were rendered blind with each passing second, but though a warrior spirit thrived in her small frame, even Raven knew their chances of surviving the battle were slim.

Henry shot three more ghouls in the face, each one becoming unrecognizable as once human, and as the bodies dropped to the ground, he heard the click of an empty weapon. Popping out the spent clip, he reached into his pocket for another only to find himself looking into the eyes of a zombie.

This one had seen better days, the flesh on its face all but peeled away, the faded bone beneath peering through. The nose was gone, only two open slits that dripped pus and mucus. One eye had rotted from the socket and the other looked like it would be joining its mate soon enough. But the ghoul could still see, and as Henry wrapped his hand around the new clip, he felt the ghoul's teeth sink into his wrist.

The teeth were like steel and he cried out, but more in revulsion than fear. Dropping the empty Glock to his feet, he reached down and drew the sixteen inch panga from its sheath riding his hip. As the zombie worried at his wrist, sinking its fetid teeth deep into his arm, Henry raised the panga and brought it down so hard it sliced the ghoul's head in twain, as if it was made of nothing more than paper.

The body dropped to the ground, but the head was still attached to his arm by clamped teeth, and as he raised his arm high, Mary let out a gasp between shots at the closing zombies, to stare at the severed head hanging from Henry's wrist. "Henry, oh God no!" Mary screamed.

"Forget about it, just keep shooting!" Henry yelled as he used the tip of the panga to pry the yellow teeth apart. As he did, the head fell away to roll between his feet, and he raised his boot and brought it down on the head, crushing it to mush as brains spilled out around the sole of his boot.

He glanced down at the wound to see it bleeding freely, and he knew what that bite meant, but for now he needed to deal with the undead, save his friends, and what happened later would be dealt with.

By his side, Jimmy fired another barrage of death at the closing horde, his blast slicing a ghoul in half. The legs continued onward for three more feet as the severed torso began to crawl across the ground, its insides dragging behind it as the other zombies stepped on its entrails and halted it, that is until the trodden feet were lifted and the ghoul could move again.

"So, Henry!" Jimmy yelled out. "How 'bout a plan that's gonna get us out of this shit!"

"I don't have one!" Henry replied.

"What?" Jimmy yelled back as he kicked a ghoul in the balls to no effect and followed it with a shot to the face. "You always have a plan!"

"Not this time, pal."

Behind Henry, Sue yelled again and Henry spun to see her surrounded by five zombies. Bending over, he picked up his Glock and quickly popped in a fresh clip, but as he looked around at his fellow companions, each one trapped in their own war with the dead, he saw only he was close enough to save her.

But as he readied the Glock and prepared to fire, he saw with that sinking feeling of dread that is absolute fact, that he was going to be too late.

Though he raised the Glock and fired four shots, two double-taps each, the remaining, fifth zombie managed to get its teeth into Sue's throat, and with a growl like an animal, it clamped down and pulled back.

As the ghoul snapped its head back, Henry was already firing and the shot took the zombie in the forehead. Its skull disappeared and its mouth fell slack as the large piece of Sue's flesh in its mouth dropped away.

Sue, reaching for her throat, turned and stared at Henry, their eyes making contact despite the carnage around them. Henry could see the blood spurting from between her fingers, and as he watched, he saw the flame die in her eyes as she slumped to the ground.

"No!" he screamed, kicking and punching the ghouls aside as he fought to reach Sue, but he knew before reaching her that it was too late. He had seen it too many times to count and he knew what would happen next, though it broke his heart to admit it.

But he didn't reach her, because before he was halfway there, half a dozen ghouls blocked his path. Firing from the hip, he shot three of them before the others came at him. He raised the panga and began dancing and darting back and forth, always moving so pale, claw-like hands couldn't seek a hold on him. As he did this, the panga was a blur, slicing hands and arms off like a scythe to wheat.

His wrist stung where he was bitten but he ignored it, concentrating on the battle at hand. He tried to peer over the sea of shifting heads, but it seemed to go on forever. As he wracked his brain to remember how the six companions had ended up trapped with no hope of escape, it eluded him, but he knew whatever predicament had gotten them here was irrelevant, the only thing that mattered was escape.

Mary fired her .38 S&W at the rotting faces that came for her, and as Henry turned, he saw three ghouls coming up from behind her, her attention focused only in front of her.

"Mary, behind you!" Henry yelled, but no sooner did he speak, then Mary was overrun by bodies. He caught sight of her scared face before she was lost under a sea of rotting corpses. He heard her scream once, more frustration than fear, and then the scream went into a high-pitched shriek, and a second later he saw her decapitated head dancing amongst the ghouls like a beach ball at a rock-and-roll concert.

"Oh, Christ, no!" Henry screamed as Mary's mouth still opened and closed, the blood seeping from the neck wound. That was when a zombie grabbed the severed head and jammed its hand into the open neck stump, pulling out the muscles and tongue from within.

Something inside Henry broke then, something that could never be fixed. Mary had been the daughter he'd never had and without her, plus Sue, now gone, there just didn't seem to be a reason to go on.

He heard yells to his left and he turned to see Jimmy and Cindy back to back, Cindy firing her M-16 on full auto as Jimmy now used his .38, his shotgun empty and hanging over his shoulder. Each of them fired into the undead crowd without stopping, but there were just too many bodies.

Henry punched a zombie away from him, then kicked another in the face, and as he managed a second of breathing room, he was able to watch as Jimmy, then Cindy, were swarmed by the dead, both fighting to the very end. Cindy was ripped in half, nails digging into her chest to tear it open. As her organs were pulled from her still heaving breast, he saw her blonde hair turn scarlet as her blood exploded out of her to bathe everything in the vicinity.

Jimmy had a rougher time as each of his limbs was grabbed by pale hands that were like small vises. He spit and yelled at the undead faces, that is until they began to sink their teeth into the joints of his arms and legs, causing him to yell out in absolute agony.

One at a time, with the flesh and material of his clothing torn by teeth, his arms and legs were separated from his torso, Jimmy was conscious the entire time, and though he begged for death or at least to pass out from shock, his mind refused to acquiesce.

As Henry raised his Glock, he locked gazes with Jimmy, and the young man yelled out, "Kill me, Henry, for Christ's sake, fucking kill me!"

With tears in his eyes, Henry raised the Glock higher, and though he couldn't save his best friend, at least he could grant him peace. One shot rang out and the 9mm round struck Jimmy between the eyes. His head snapped back and his eyes closed, the ghouls never ceasing their feeding.

Henry felt something tug on his left leg and he looked down to see that a zombie had crawled up to him. It was the one Jimmy had blown in half, and it had crept up like a soldier in the forest. Before Henry could kick it away, its teeth clamped down on his left calf, sinking in to the bone and causing Henry to cry out.

With the panga in his hand, he brought it down like he was chopping wood and the blade sank into the skull more than halfway, the head ceasing to bite him but now trapping his blade in the bone.

As he tried to free it, he spotted Raven through a crowd of zombies. She was like a dervish, bouncing from place to place, her hands slashing at any ghoul stupid enough to come too close. But then she met a zombie her nails had no effect on. The ghoul had been a member of SWAT when he had lived and he was still decked out in riot gear. His face was nothing but a white skull and Henry knew this ghoul was one of the originals. This dead man must have been caught out in the rain back when it was still deadly and had died only to come back as one of the undead.

As the ghoul came at Raven, her nails did nothing to its armored body, the Kevlar able to stop a high impact round, let alone a teenage girl with fingernails for weapons, no matter how sharp.

As Raven fought off the zombie, it came at her and grabbed her by the throat. She kicked and scratched at its eyes, taking out both of them, but the ghoul never ceased its attack. It didn't need eyes to kill her, and once its hands were locked onto her, she couldn't escape. As she became trapped, more ghouls surrounded her, and as Henry watched helplessly, Raven was torn apart by teeth and nails. He spotted her ebony hair once in the crowd of the dead, and then she was lost from sight. He realized the entire time the ghouls killed her, she never so much as screamed once. She had always been quiet and had stayed that way to the end.

Henry was alone now, the only one remaining, and as he let go of the hilt of the panga, realizing he couldn't free it from the zombie's skull, the mouth still clamped on his leg, he fired the last rounds in his Glock.

As he was surrounded, he fired the last bullet into a pale face and then raised his fists, prepared to take as many of the undead bastards with him as he could.

But as he kicked and punched, he spun around and then halted, too shocked to strike the ghoul before him.

For the ghoul was none other than Sue. Her flesh was pale now, the jagged wound in her throat still seeping blood. Because of the wound, her head was slanted to the side, her teeth now bloody and clacking up and down as her dead eyes stared at Henry.

His fist had stopped an inch from her face, and though he knew it wasn't her any longer, he just couldn't hit her. For he loved her, even in death.

And what was the point? All his friends were dead and he was bitten, soon to either turn or he would eat a bullet to spare himself the suffering to come.

"Sue, I'm sorry, I told you I would always protect you," he said as the undead surrounded him and hands reached out and wrapped around his body, fingers grabbing at his face. "I failed you, and I give up."

If she understood what he was telling her, she gave no inclination, but instead dove in, and with mouth open wide, prepared to rip his throat out.

He closed his eyes and prepared for the end, but at the last second, his instinct to live overrode his sorrow and he opened his eyes and pushed her away. Punching and kicking, he fought his way through the horde, never ceasing his movement. He felt teeth take bites from his flesh again and again but each time he made it a foot further from the horde.

But though he fought a valiant battle, he tripped over his own feet and fell to the ground, and when he rolled onto his back, he found himself staring up at his five friends. Mary was there, her severed head now held in her hands, her torso nothing but a gaping cavity. Jimmy was there, too, his arms and legs missing as he rolled across the ground, a jagged black hole in his forehead. Raven came up next to him, her body torn and ravaged by dozens of teeth and hands, and then Cindy came up behind Mary, her body all but unrecognizable, only her blonde hair letting him know it was her. And in the middle of the pack, was Sue, her body now ruined and mutilated.

As his undead friends closed in on him, Henry raised his hands up to stop them, but their open mouths, dripping with blood, came forward, blotting out the night and smothering him, as if he was in a blanket.

He couldn't breathe and he felt the air grow hot, his arms trapped like he was tied up, and as he let out a scream, he jumped up, tossing the blanket off him to stare around the dark room, only the one small candle in the far corner to break the absolute blackness.

Jimmy glanced up from his post at the window where he was playing solitaire to see Henry looking around frantically.

"Hey, old man, you all right? You look like you just saw a ghost."

"I, uh, Jimmy, you're okay." He turned his head to see his other friends also alive, each sleeping silently. To his left, lying beside him, was Sue, her eyes closed as she slept. As Henry's heart slowed its frantic beating in his chest, he blinked the fear away and stood up, leaving his bedroll where it was spread out on the floor.

"Of course I'm okay, why wouldn't I be?" Jimmy asked as he looked at Henry with a quizzical look. "Hey, you're not getting senile in your old age, are you? I mean, more than usual."

Henry rubbed his face with his hands, the images of his nightmare falling away, and he shook his head no. "I'm fine, I just thought..." he waved his right hand in a *forget it* gesture. "Never mind."

He went to the corner they had decided would be used for a bathroom and he pissed in the small hole in the floor. There had been a collapse in the foundation and the large crack had become exposed. It was as close to an outhouse as they could ask for and it would do until the next day when they planned on heading out again.

"How is it outside?" he asked Jimmy as he zipped up his fly.

As he turned to look at his young friend, Jimmy shrugged. "The storm's slowing down and with luck we can head out in the morning, like you said,"

Henry nodded. "That's good." He stared at Jimmy, the image of his friend with no arms or legs pressing in his mind and he shook the vision away. "Look, I'm up now so why don't I take over for you."

"You sure? You've got another hour before you have to relieve me."

"Nah, go 'head and grab some sleep, I've got this," Henry said with a smile.

"Okay, fine," Jimmy said and jogged across the room, took off his boots, and was under the bedroll with Cindy in less than a second. She grunted and yelled at him, saying his hands were cold and to leave her alone, and he chuckled like a school boy. Then the two settled down and were quiet.

Henry let his eyes play over his sleeping friends as his nightmare flashed across his mind, and he realized though he tried not to admit it, those fears had always been there. His worst possible nightmare was seeing his friends torn apart or worse, and though he tried to keep those feelings repressed, there were times he couldn't leave them bottled up.

He supposed it might have had to do with the fact he was hungry. Hell, they were all hungry.

After leaving the mountains of Colorado, they had found themselves in the middle of an early snowstorm. Luckily, they had found a small hunting cabin and for more than two weeks had been holed up inside its worn walls as their meager supplies of food had waned.

But now it looked like the storm was finally passing, and the hope was that in the morning, they could set out and seek food. Though water was in abundance thanks to the frozen snow, they still needed food and he knew whether the storm ended in the morning or not, they would have to set out or else they would end up too weak from hunger to leave later.

He reached inside his jacket and took out a small map he'd found in the cabin. It was hand drawn and Henry was fairly certain the owner of the cabin had illustrated it. It showed what the owner had believed was good hunting grounds, as well as where the best natural paths were. Henry didn't know how reliable the map was but seems they were lost, it was better than wandering around aimlessly until they died of exposure. Folding the map neatly, he slipped it back into his pocket.

As he pulled his jacket closer around him and stared out at the high snow drifts, the wind howling like a banshee, he did something he didn't do often, as he felt the situation was just that desperate.

He prayed.

Hours later, with the storm finally abated, the companions set out across the snow-covered landscape.

Because the storm had come so early in the season, it wasn't that much of a surprise when the sun came out and began to warm the land. But no sooner did the sun appear than it was lost behind thick clouds that looked as if they would open up once more at a moment's notice. A light drizzle began to fall, and with the temperature rising slightly, the snow turned to slush in many places, soaking each of the companions' boots. The slush splashed when they walked and soon they were all miserable.

"This sucks," Jimmy said flatly, summing it up for the rest of them.

But with little choice, they marched on, avoiding the deeper drifts as Henry used his panga to feel the frozen ground ahead of them.

"Shit, I'm so hungry I think I'm gonna eat my boots before the day is through," Jimmy said as he trotted behind Henry, Cindy by his side.

"Just hang in there, Jimmy," Henry said. "Our luck has got to change soon."

"Hey, Henry, heads up," Raven called as she pointed to the left.

Henry turned to see four zombies stumbling over a rise, plowing through the snowdrifts as if the snow wasn't there. Henry had to admit, right now, he envied the dead just a little as he pulled his collar tighter around his neck. Being dead, the ghouls felt no cold and the snow was nothing but a nuisance to them.

"I thought the deaders would freeze in the snow," Jimmy commented.

Mary nodded. "You're right, but it's not cold enough yet."

"You think they'll just freeze up till spring?" Jimmy asked.

"I don't know," Mary replied. "From what we've seen so far, yeah, but no one's been able to find out for sure. They go dormant it seems and then wake up when the snow begins to melt and the temperature rises."

"Still, we could just go somewhere like Alaska and live there till they all rot away." He turned to Henry and called out, "What do you think, Henry? How 'bout going to Antarctica, maybe?"

Henry chuckled. "Sure, Jimmy, just hop onboard my flying carpet and I'll run you right over there. Maybe if we can find a plane and someone to fly it we could give it a try, but until then we're stuck in the good old U S of A.

The ghouls were closer now, and they let out a moan, their noses and brows dripping with small icicles. Jimmy raised his shotgun to take them out when Henry reached out and pushed down the barrel.

"What are you doing, Jimmy? You fire that shotgun and anything in a mile radius or more will know we're out here. No, we gotta take 'em out with silence. You up for it?"

Jimmy grinned as he spun the shotgun around and prepared to use the butt like a club. "Bring it on, Henry. I'm always ready for a good fight."

Henry looked at the girls. "We got this, ladies, you stay here."

Mary crossed her arms over her chest as she shifted her feet in the snow. "Oh, thank God we have you big strong men to take care of us, what would we ever do without you?"

"Why, you think you could do better?" Jimmy asked, the zombies now only twenty feet away and closing.

Cindy stepped up and pushed Jimmy to the side as she handed him her M-16. "Just watch us, sport," she said and looked to Mary, Sue and Raven. "Shall we girls?"

"Ah, I'll stay here with the men, if it's all right," Sue said. "I'm not much on fighting, you guys know that."

"Suit yourself," Cindy shrugged.

Mary, Cindy and Raven stepped away from the rest of the group and made their way towards the zombies.

"You think they'll be okay?" Jimmy asked Henry as he watched the women move away and up the slope the zombies were on.

Henry chuckled. "Are you kidding me? I feel kinda bad for the deaders now."

Cindy was in the lead, followed by Mary and Raven. As she walked up the slope, she let her eyes take in the condition of the four approaching zombies.

They were a decrepit quartet, that was for sure, and Cindy wondered if they were some of the originals from when the rains first came.

Nearly two years later and the first people to die and reanimate were still shambling around what was left of America. The cities were the worst and had picked up the nickname, deadlands. Only fools went close to cities, and most who did never returned.

Cindy let her eyes play over the first ghoul in line. It was female, she could tell, but that was where the identification ended. The face was rotted to the point there was no flesh left and the hair on the scalp had fallen out long ago. The clothes were so filthy and matted with blood and dried gore that Cindy couldn't tell the make or style of the outfit. Most of the material was nothing but rags and more brown, dried and rotting flesh peeked through.

The second ghoul was in the same shape as the first, only this one had been a man. It was obvious due to the size of the ghoul's arm and width of the shoulders. The face was in a similar state of disrepair; only this one still had a nose, though by the looks of it the nose wouldn't be there for too much longer if it was allowed to wander away.

The third and fourth zombies were also sexless, both of medium height with matted, greasy hair and milky-white eyes that seemed to see nothing, yet everything at the same time.

"How are we going to do this, girls?" Mary asked as she pulled a hunting knife from a sheath on her hip. Her brown hair, past her shoulders, blew out behind her in the wind. Her cheeks were red from the cold and her eyes wide with the excitement of battle and she was a far cry from the secretary who had once worked in the lobby of Pineridge Labs.

Cindy had also pulled a knife from her waist, an eight inch, razor-sharp blade to be exact, and she gripped the hilt tighter.

Raven spoke up, cutting off Cindy. "I'll take the big one, you two can have the other three."

Mary glanced at Raven to see the sixteen-year-old's face was serious. Raven was so taciturn and this was a long speech for her. Ever since meeting Raven, Mary had tried to get to know her better but each time Raven had politely refused. Mary quietly realized she knew as much about Raven now as she did when first meeting her and Sue after finding them inside a bus the companions had stolen from a tribe of cannibals.

But Mary also knew though lacking in personal information, she trusted Raven with her life and had done so on many occasions. The young girl was an excellent fighter and could kill with nothing more than her hands, thanks to her long fingernails which were sharpened to razor tips.

"Okay, fine. Mary, you and me will take the three on the left and Raven can have the big one," Cindy said and looked Raven in the face. "You sure?"

Raven only nodded, her long, ink black hair blowing out behind her, looking for all purposes like she wore a cape.

Mary touched her .38, just wanting to know it was there. Cindy carried a small sidearm as well, but both knew if they had to use them, then anyone in the area would be alerted to their presence. Plus, she didn't want to have to fall back on using her gun, for if she did, it would only help perpetuate the stereotype that she and Cindy needed help by the men.

After all they been through together, Mary still shook her head each time Henry tried to coddle her. She knew he only did it because he was overprotective, but still, after all the battles she had fought with him, she would think he would consider her an equal by now.

The ghouls were only a few feet away and the wind shifted, causing the aroma of rotting meat to touch Mary's nose.

Mary exhaled through her nose to then begin to suck in air through her mouth. She was used to the redolence of death, but that didn't mean she welcomed it.

Before she was close enough to deal with one of the ghouls, Raven suddenly took off at a sprint, dashing past her and Cindy as she headed toward the large zombie like a heat seeking missile.

The zombie moaned loudly and raised it hands to grab Raven, its teeth already preparing to tear her apart, but as Raven reached the ghoul, she darted to the left, the zombie overreaching her and falling into the snow. Raven spun around like a gymnast and jumped onto the back of the ghoul, her arms wrapping around the zombie's face, her fingernails pointed directly at its eyes.

In one fluid movement, she stabbed both eyes with the index finger on each hand, her nails slicing into the milky-white orbs like a hot knife through butter. Though the ghoul felt no pain, it sensed the world go dark, and it reached up and grabbed Raven by her jacket, pulling her off its back with one yank of its large arm.

She fell into the snow, sliding for a few feet, until she rolled onto her side and popped back up. She turned to see Mary and Cindy reach her and she grinned widely as she shook ice crystals from her hair.

"That should slow the bastard down," she said proudly.

Both Mary and Cindy nodded, then looked back at the oncoming zombies. The large one, now blind, had grabbed the female zombie and was tearing the ghoul apart with its meaty paws.

The three women watched silently as the large ghoul pulled the female zombie's arms off and raised one limb to its mouth, chomping down messily. But as soon as it tasted the decayed meat, it spit it out, resembling a child who didn't like what he had eaten.

Tossing the limb away, it stumbled away to disappear over a snow drift, its moans and crashing carrying on the wind before it was lost from sight.

Mary and Cindy weren't listening however as they still had two healthy zombies plus an armless one to deal with.

"Mary, you go left and I'll go right. Raven, take care of the one with no arms," Cindy told them as the women charged at the ghouls, their blades held high.

Mary was the first to dispatch her opponent. As the arms of the ghoul reached for her, she knocked them aside and jammed her knife into the milky-white left eye. She felt the tip slide into the eye socket, grating on the sides of the skull to plunge into the brain. The ghoul twitched for half a heartbeat and then dropped to the snow, very dead.

Raven was next, and she snap-kicked the female ghoul in the chest, knocking it into the snow. She followed the kick with a jump onto its torso, where she reached down, placed a hand on each side of its head, and twisted sharply, snapping the neck and severing the spinal cord. The ghoul's legs immediately stopped moving, though the head was still active. Still, it was harmless and forgotten as she rolled to her feet.

Cindy wasn't as lucky and had a bout of misfortune as she reached her zombie. Mimicking Mary, she had knocked the out-reaching arms aside and was about to plunge her knife into a milky eye when her right foot came down on a patch of ice that was hidden under the snow. As her arm was raised for the killing blow, she found her feet and legs swinging out from under her as she fell onto her back, her body horizontal for a brief moment before gravity pulled her to the earth. She landed so hard she had the wind knocked out of her, and she blinked to clear the fog that descended over her mind.

As she shook her head, she looked up to see the zombie she was about to kill coming at her, the head directly in a path for her face.

In the brief instant before the ghoul would land on her, she realized no matter how fast she moved, it wasn't going to be quick enough to save herself. As if it was in slow motion, she saw the ghoul falling onto her, its mouth opening wide, as it got ready to sink its yellowed teeth into her nose or cheek.

All she could do is close her eyes and wait for the inevitable pain, knowing once bit, she would end up on the last train west.

As the zombie leaned down to sink its teeth into Cindy's face, she heard a sharp crack of a gun, the report rolling across the hills like thunder, causing a few birds in a nearby tree to take flight. She recognized it instantly; it was Henry's Glock. No sooner did the sound of the gunshot reach her, then a loud squelching sound overrode it and she felt bits of bone and brains splash onto her face, the snow around her head turning a dark shade of brown thanks to the rotting brains.

Half of the zombie's head was blown off and the body twitched on top of Cindy, before going slack and dropping onto her like a spent lover.

As she felt a gelatinous substance ooze near her lips, she opened her eyes to see the zombie was very dead.

Jimmy was only a few feet from her now, and before she could move, he was grabbing the zombie by the scruff of its collar and yanking it away from her, tossing it to the side like errant trash.

"Cindy, are you okay?" Jimmy asked, the worry in his voice apparent to her.

She nodded, feeling a piece of brain slide into her collar and touch her neck. "Yeah, I'm fine. Where's Henry?"

"Here," Henry replied while walking up to her. He stopped when he was four feet away, looking down on her as Jimmy crouched beside her, touching her hair tenderly with his gloved hand.

"Thank you, Henry. I don't even want to think about what might have happened."

He waved her gratitude away. "Don't worry about it, honey. Hell, you've saved me enough times; it's nice to return the favor."

"Are you sure you're okay?" Jimmy asked her again.

"I will be if you'll help me up. There's snow in my pants and my butt is freezing."

"Huh? Oh, yeah, sure, sorry," Jimmy said and pulled her to her feet. She used her sleeve to wipe her face clean, Jimmy picking away a few choice gobbets that had stuck to her hair.

Mary and Raven joined them, as did Sue, who saw the action was over for the time being.

Mary grabbed Cindy's arm and squeezed it, the gesture saying she was glad her friend was unharmed.

"So much for us women being mighty warriors," Cindy said, embarrassed by what had happened, as she cleaned off the rest of the brain matter. "I can't believe I let some ice almost get me killed."

"Hey, speak for yourself," Raven said. She had kicked butt and she knew it.

"Don't beat yourself up, Cindy," Henry said. "It happens; next time be more careful. Remember, when fighting in the snow, ice can be anywhere." He grinned as she touched her shoulder like a father. "Besides, that's why you have us...to watch your back."

"And backside," Jimmy grinned lecherously trying to shake off the worry he'd been feeling. When he saw her fall, his heart had skipped a beat. After being with Cindy for more than a year, he couldn't imagine life without her. He made a mental note to tell her as much when they were alone later that night.

Cindy smiled. "That's my Jimmy, always thinking of sex."

Henry clapped his gloved hands to get their attention. "All right, people, Cindy's fine and we need to keep moving. That shot I took will alert anything in the area we're here, and when it arrives, I want to be long gone."

They each gathered themselves and turned to head out, but as they passed the zombie Raven had paralyzed, Jimmy took an extra second to stomp on its still animated head. The heavy sole of his right boot heel came down on the decayed forehead, pushing it deep into the snow. Jimmy raised his boot again, and when he brought it down, he used the rear edge of the heel.

The heel caved in the face, shattering the jaw and puncturing one eye, but it still didn't destroy the brain. But without a mouth and only one eye, the head could do no damage if an unwary traveler came across it. Plus, Jimmy liked to dish out what he hoped was pain to a zombie whenever possible. If he had his way, he would kill every one he came across, though he knew that was impossible. There was simply not enough ammunition in the world to get the job done.

"Was that really necessary?" Cindy asked as she walked beside Jimmy. She was wiggling a little, trying to get the ice out of her ass crack. It was already melting and that helped, but now the rear of her pants and lower part of her shirt under her jackets was wet.

She was already looking forward to when they could build a fire so she could dry off.

"Yeah, it was," Jimmy said as if that settled the matter.

Looking around as they walked away from the destroyed ghouls, Henry said, "I hope there aren't any more roamers in the area."

"If there are, we'll deal with 'em, old man," Jimmy replied. "And next time we'll use our guns, and what happens, happens. This stealth shit almost got my girl killed."

"Jimmy," Cindy said, wanting him to stop, but Henry raised his hand for her not to continue.

"No, it's okay, Cindy, he has a point, though I still think silence is better. Besides, we all know Jimmy, shoot first and deal with the aftermath when it comes."

"No way, not Jimmy," Mary said sarcastically. "Why, he's the most level-headed among us."

"Hey, that was a crack against me, wasn't it," Jimmy said, not quite getting he was the butt of a silent joke.

"Oh, no, baby," Cindy said. "Mary meant what she said. You're the most practical one in our little group. We all want to be more like you."

"Well, I should hope you would, I..." then Jimmy stopped as he figured out Cindy had a wide smile and was messing with him. As he looked at the others, each wore a wide grin, that is except for Raven who was not paying attention but instead was watching their surroundings.

Jimmy frowned deeply. "Hey, that's not funny, quit pickin' on me!" He said it like a middle-schooler who was being made fun of by his friends.

Cindy began to laugh and soon the others were, too, Henry slapping Jimmy on the back.

Cindy came up and kissed a pouting Jimmy on the cheek. "Don't worry, lover, you're still my man," she said so only he could hear. "And I'll prove it tonight if we can get a chance to be alone and find a place that's warm. That perked him up, and as his cheeks turned a deeper shade of red, the group climbed a snow dune and trekked deeper into the forest.

A full five minutes passed before the first of the coyotes appeared from the surrounding brush and trees.

Their muzzles sniffed the air but there was no longer the scent of the six humans.

They had been attracted to the fight between the women and the zombies, but were too scared to come out of hiding.

The last time the pack had tried to attack humans, two of their number had been shot. So they had lied in wait, hoping one of the humans might be left behind, perhaps a weak one in the group.

As they padded out onto flattened snow made by the companions' feet, they slowly crept up to the destroyed ghouls, carefully sniffing to make sure they were truly dead. As they crept closer with heads down, they prepared to run at a moment's notice.

Eventually, they came to the conclusion that the zombies were inactive, and as the leader went in and tore some of the decayed meat from a shoulder blade, the others quickly followed suit.

The meat might be old, but it was sustenance, and in the harsh winter the coyotes had learned to adapt.

Ripping and tearing at the corpses, they fought over what scraps remained on the bodies, the circle of life ever revolving.

* * *

Mid-afternoon, hours after the battle with the ghouls, the six travelers came upon a small glade. The wind had scoured the area clear of snow, though the south side had snow piled more than five feet high. It was still an excellent place to rest and build a fire.

After Jimmy and Cindy gathered what wood they could find buried under the snow, the pickings slim, Henry pulled out a package of fine-mesh steel wool. This was his last bag, the other three he'd found in a hardware store at the last town they'd gone through, the bags now gone, having been used, and he was glad for this remaining one.

As he began to separate the mesh into a wider cloud of wool, it parted, and he reached inside his jacket and took out a 9-volt battery.

"Here ya go, Henry, this is all we could find," Jimmy said as he and Cindy walked up with a few sticks and twigs.

"It'll have to do," he said as they dropped the kindling into a small circle dug in the frozen ground.

"Need any help?" Mary asked.

"No, thanks, I can do it," Henry replied.

When the kindling was set up, he took the top of the 9-volt, the leads exposed, and began to touch it to the steel wool. Almost immediately the wool began to glow and soon it was burning. When he had it going as well as possible, he set it into the kindling, then added a few pieces of newspaper taken from his pack to help get the blaze going.

Sue and Raven gathered close, each of them hoping the fire wouldn't go out, for they had been traveling for hours and all were cold and needed to rest.

"Come on, baby, you can do it," Jimmy coaxed the flames as he leaned in closer, feeling the first hint of warmth.

It looked like it would go out, the kindling too wet from being in the snow, but then it began to snap and crackle and the flames grew hotter. Henry, feeling desperate, took a handkerchief out of his backpack and set it into the fire. This was enough to add to the blaze to get it going and all sighed with relief as the flames began to burn with more strength.

Soon, the fire was casting a circle of warmth as each of them surrounded it, warming their hands and face as the heat penetrated their clothes to their chilled bodies.

"This is the last one, guys, after this we freeze," Henry said, referring to the steel wool.

"Shit, Henry," Jimmy grunted. "There's got to be an end to this damn forest, we've been walking forever."

"I hope you're right about that, Jimmy," Henry said. "Or else they're gonna find six frozen bodies in the spring."

"Oh, Henry, you're so morose," Sue said as she snuggled up next to him. "We'll be fine, you need to have faith."

"A little luck wouldn't hurt either," Mary added as she rubbed her arms.

"Sue, the only faith I have is in myself and you guys, my family. Anything else is up for grabs."

"So, what? We just keep walking and hope for the best?" Jimmy asked.

Henry nodded, the fire turning his cheeks a shade of red. He had taken off his hat and his white hair, once damp from sweat, was now drying. The ash-gray hair still had a few strands of brown in it, but over the past two years, since the dead began to walk, it had almost turned completely gray; which added to Jimmy's affectionate nickname of 'old man' all the more fitting.

Henry shook his head as he used a branch to stir the flames. He wasn't looking forward to leaving the warmth of the fire and trekking on, but he knew soon that was what he and the others would need to do if they wanted to survive the frozen wasteland he and his friends now found themselves in.

"I'm afraid that's all we can do, Jimmy," Henry replied.

"And what if we don't find anything out here? It could be miles before we come across something to help us. What if there are no towns or cabins like the one we just left?" Jimmy pushed.

Henry paused before speaking, as if he was considering the answer. He looked each of the companions in the eye, and said very simply, as if he was chatting about the weather, "Then we die."

Jimmy blamed the map, but Henry blamed Jimmy. Mary blamed the snow and Cindy said it was just bad luck. Sue tried to support everyone and Raven had no opinion other than that she was hungry.

Secretly, Henry was wondering if they would have been better off staying back at the cabin, for though they would have run out of food and possibly starved to death eventually, at least they could have done so in a relatively warm environment.

Though blame was tossed around left and right, at the end it didn't change the fact that they were very lost.

The sun had disappeared for good, now replaced by heavy clouds that looked as if they were going to open up at any second. With nothing else to do but go on, the six companions trudged through the snowy wasteland, their heads down and jackets pulled tightly around them.

As dusk was falling, and Henry was searching for a spot they could set up a cold camp—something he wasn't relishing—the group found themselves in a region of steep, but shallow valleys, where the drifts of snow covered only one side, allowing the walking to be much easier.

Though they trudged on, Henry tried to console himself with the fact that they weren't truly 'lost'. He knew if he wanted to, and the others agreed, they could turn around and trek back to the cabin again. But he also knew that was a mistake, despite their dire circumstances.

Their only chance at survival was to continue forward.

As the clouds opened up with a cold, driving rain, each of them hunched over just a little more, trudging on.

Soon, snow was replaced by slush and all their boots were soaked through. Though military grade footwear, the boots couldn't handle complete immersion for so long, and more often than not, one of them would step into a puddle that turned out to be a small pond, more than a foot deep.

As they continued on, Henry decided stopping would be foolhardy, so they walked for the entire night, six ambiguous shapes blending in to the shadows of the darkness.

They had seen no other signs of life, human or animal, and they all felt as if they had fallen back in time to a place on earth where life didn't exist yet.

Many times, in the darkness, they found their path blocked by heavy snow or land fall and they would have to retrace their steps until they could find a way around the altercation, and the constant exertion was tiring them out to the point each of them looked as if they would fall down, to never rise again.

Even Henry's indefatigable spirit was waning, and with Sue on his arm as he helped her walk, he wondered just how long it would be before the first of them fell over in exhaustion.

Finally, with the night half over, they came upon a large copse of trees with dense branches standing alone at the base of a hill. As they gathered under the trees, huddling together for what little warmth they could take from one another, the rain still fell, turning the ground to slippery mud and freezing them to the bone.

The temperature dropped once more, close to freezing this time, and it was one of the worst nights any of them could ever remember having to endure. Sleep wasn't an option, as each of them needed to stay awake and focused. Jogging in place was the favorite activity, and all wished desperately for a fire, but with everything soaked through, it wasn't an option.

It was one of the longest nights any of them could ever recall living through.

Eventually, dawn arrived, and as the sun touched the gray sky, the rain finally ceased, though a heavy drizzle persisted.

Without saying a word to one another, the companions moved on, their clothes soaked thoroughly and frostbite only hours away.

Jimmy fell back to walk with Henry and Sue, and as the others plodded on, he whispered so only they could hear him. "Cindy's not doing so good, Henry," he said. "We need to stop and get a fire going."

"Yeah, I know, but if you see anything that'll burn, I'm all for it," he replied as he gestured to the sodden trees and brush, the mud and slush all around them.

"Tell me about it," Jimmy replied. "But I'm just sayin', if we can't get warmed up soon...I'm worried about her, Henry."

"Look, Jimmy, we're all in a bad way. Don't you think I'd stop and do that if we could? Just keep an eye out, maybe something will come along soon."

Jimmy nodded, knowing Henry was right, and he picked up his pace and caught up with Cindy. She leaned on him and he helped her along. Mary and Raven walked side by side, though neither spoke. Henry could see Mary's face and where her skin was once vibrant and fresh, it was now pale and her face drawn. He had no doubt he looked the same.

With no other options, he pushed on, hugging Sue tighter as he helped her through the mud.

It was mid-afternoon when Jimmy, on point, came across something of interest to him. Holding up his hand, he went off the natural path and slowed when he came to what looked like a large boulder covered in wet snow.

"What are you doing?" Henry called out as he watched Jimmy stepping through the foot high snow. All of them were about ready to fall over for good. Even Raven looked to be at the end of her rope. All their bellies were full of snow, but even with all the water they could consume, they were still undernourished and needed food. As Henry watched, Jimmy moved through the snow to stop in front of the large drift, and he wondered if his friend was seeing things, perhaps had gone crazy.

"I saw a reflection, Henry, like metal, just give me a second," Jimmy called as he began to study the snow pile. The others had now stopped and each of them wanted to sit down, but all knew if they did, they would probably never get up again. Henry could feel the tips of his fingers going numb and the end of his nose tingling, and knew frostbite was just around the corner. That is if he didn't have it already.

"Ha! I knew it!" Jimmy cried out as he began to brush at the snow pile.

"What's he doing?" Sue asked Henry.

"He's gone nuts," Mary said as she hugged herself. Her cheeks were so red she looked like a Christmas tree ornament, her breath fogging out in a white cloud as she breathed.

As Henry watched Jimmy brushing at the snow pile, he quickly realized there was something of color underneath the snow other than a boulder. He saw the color green!

"No, I think Jimmy found something," Henry said and trudged through the snow to join him. Together, the two began brushing at the object under the snow until more than half of it was exposed.

As the two men worked, the four women joined them, helping where they could until Cindy declared, "It's a car!"

"So?" Mary said. "If it's out here in the middle of nowhere, I doubt it still runs. And even if it did, there're no roads to drive it on."

Henry finished wiping off the trunk and he turned to Mary. "You're right, Mary, but if there's a car here then there has to be a road nearby. We just can't see it because of the all the slush and snow."

"Good point, old man," Jimmy cracked. "But I was hoping maybe we could get it started and have some heat."

Henry's eyes lit up at the possibility. "Well, let's see what we can do, then." He turned to the women. "Come on, ladies, help us out. If Jimmy's right, we can get it running and sit inside and enjoy some warmth."

Though the women all made a face, they joined in and five minutes later the car was exposed.

Mary called out that it was a Toyota when she brushed off the medallion on the license plate, the top of the plate establishing the car had been bought at Al's Toyota dealership in Detroit.

"Detroit? Man, this car's a long way from him," Jimmy said as he finished brushing off the trunk and went to the driver's door. "Let's see if its unlocked." Pressing the button on the door handle, the door popped open and snow fell into the interior from where it had been in the rain well.

Jimmy, not wasting time, climbed inside and called out, "Hey, the keys are still in it, too!"

It was then that he detected the stink of rot and decay, and as he glanced at the rearview mirror, he saw the pale, desiccated, half-frozen face glaring back at him...just before it snapped forward, yellow teeth ready to bite.

The next three seconds passed in slow motion for Jimmy. As he considered what was happening, his mind went in two different directions as he weighed the outcome of his next action.

If the zombie managed to bite him, then he knew he was dead. First infection, then weakness, then death, to be followed by his return. Of course, he knew Henry wouldn't let that happen to him and that his friend would put a bullet in his head to spare him from walking around as one of the things.

He thought of Cindy and how sad she'd be when he died, and about how his body would be left buried in the snow somewhere and in the spring, when the thaw began, he would become exposed to then become nothing but meat to the scavengers of the forest.

In the blink of an eye, he decided he didn't like that outcome, so as the zombie's head snapped forward, its mouth open wide to take a bite out of him, Jimmy spun around and used his arm as a muzzle, jamming it into the ghoul's mouth. Fetid teeth clamped down hard on his arm but the thick material of his jacket prevented his flesh from being torn, though he did feel the pressure of the front teeth.

Without thinking, his instincts honed after two years of fighting the dead, he reached down with his free hand and pulled his nine inch Bowie knife from the sheath on his hip.

As the ghoul worried at his arm like a dog to a bone, Jimmy brought his arm around and jammed the knife into the zombie's ear. The blade slid in like a warm knife into butter, the blade hesitating for a moment before puncturing cartilage and penetrating the brain. The ghoul began to twitch in spastic movements as Jimmy forced the blade deeper.

To make sure of his kill, he twisted the knife to the right, carving the brains to mush. The teeth let go and the zombie fell back onto the rear seat, like a tired passenger on a long drive.

Henry was reaching into the car now, his eyes wide with surprise. With the ice covering the windows, they had all been caught off guard, the zombie hidden from view.

"Jimmy, are you all right?" Henry asked.

Jimmy lowered his arm, looking at the indentation where the ghoul's teeth had left an impression in his jacket sleeve, and he nodded. "Yeah, Henry, I'm fine, got damn lucky, though."

Jimmy climbed out of the car and Cindy ran into his arms. She had seen it happen and was helpless to do anything as the event had happened so fast.

"I'm okay," he told her. "Got careless is all."

Mary walked up next to him. "Thought we were going to lose you, Jimmy. Who would I have to tease then?"

"Don't worry, Mary, I'm not going anywhere. Hey, if I did, then there wouldn't be anyone around to give you a hard time, right?" he chuckled.

"Right," she said and squeezed his shoulder with a smile on her lips.

Henry was dragging the dead zombie out of the car, and he tossed it a little ways to the side, the body landing in a heap. The corpse wore a flannel shirt, jeans, and a down vest. Its boots were tiny, giving him the impression the zombie had been a teenager, probably male. Sue came up to him and they both gazed down at the corpse.

"I wonder who he was," she said, always the mother hen. "Was he alive when he became trapped inside the car? Then turned later? How horrible, to die alone like that."

Henry shifted to look at her, turning her around slowly to see the others as they milled about Jimmy, glad he was okay. Raven said something that had Jimmy laughing and Cindy and Mary joined in. Raven only smiled, subdued as ever.

"See that, Sue? That's all I care about right now. This deader, it's the past. I don't care who it was or why it was out here. Them, and you, that's all that matters to me."

She smiled and kissed his cheek, feeling the scruff of his forming beard on her lips. Splashed with gray, it gave him a look of wisdom.

"I understand what you're saying," she said.

"Good, now let's get back to the others, I want to see if this car can help us or not."

Henry studied the vehicle as he moved around to look into the car now that it was empty. "Maybe some campers owned it. Figured they could leave the keys in the ignition if they were camping or hiking in the area. After all, who would've known it was here?

Hell, maybe that deader was one of them and he died and got trapped inside."

Jimmy was in the driver's seat again and he looked at Henry as he placed his hand on the ignition key still in the steering column. "I don't care how it got inside, I'm just glad it's dead. So, you ready for me to try this?"

"Go for it," Henry told him.

Jimmy closed his eyes briefly and his lips moved, fog blowing out of his nose as he breathed. To Henry it looked as if Jimmy was saying a silent prayer. Jimmy opened his eyes and turned the key, but there was nothing. Not so much as a click. He turned it off and tried again, as if that would magically charge the battery, and when still nothing happened, he punched the steering wheel, no horn sounding when his gloved fist hit the center of it.

"Damn it, I swear we're the unluckiest people on the fucking planet."

Henry pushed off from the car, looking at the women. "No go," he said sadly.

"So what now?" Mary asked. "Do we keep going?"

Henry leaned against the car again as he considered for a moment, then his brow furrowed as his mind worked. Countless times in the past, Henry had managed to get them out of tough scrapes with clever ideas and wild plans. Able to think on his feet, he could look at a problem and come up with a solution almost instantly. Sometimes the plans were more dangerous than the problem at hand, but so far he had managed to keep his people alive, so when Mary saw that look on his face, she took a step closer to him.

"I know that look, Henry, what's going on in that mind of yours?"

He pulled his panga and he stood tall. "I'll tell you in a second. It won't matter if it's empty." He then went to Jimmy. "Pop the hood, will ya, buddy?"

"Why?"

"Just do it, and save the twenty questions for later, all right?"

Jimmy shrugged and did what Henry wanted.

Henry went to the hood, opened it, and peered inside. A standard engine, everything looked to be there. He quickly took off the air filter, using the plastic covering that encased the filter, then he went to the fuse box and did the same. The fuse box was square and the covering, when flipped upside down, resembled a rectangular bowl. Then he slammed the hood closed and went to the back of the car. Going to his knees, he began to use the fuse box cover as a shovel and dug out the snow. When he was through a few minutes later, he was able to crawl under the rear bumper, leaving the fuse box cover in the snow.

Everyone watched as he used his panga to puncture the lowest part of the gas tank. It was made of plastic and it took him a few scrapings and twisting of the tip, but a few minutes later, now colder than ever, he managed to make a small hole.

No sooner did the panga slice into the gas tank, then a slow trickle of gas began to seep out of it.

"Hey, give me that fuse box cover, hurry!" he yelled as Mary went and kicked it under for him. He took it and began fidgeting under the car some more, and when he called out for the air filter cover, Sue was there to hand it to him.

The five friends stood for another seven minutes while Henry worked under the rear of the car. All were freezing and wanted desperately to get moving, if for nothing else than to move their bodies to generate some body heat.

Then, Henry began to crawl out, and after he did, he reached back under and slid out the two plastic car parts.

"Jimmy, come take one of these, will ya!" Henry called out as he went to his knees. His back and legs were covered in snow and the slush had soaked him to the bone once more. He could already feel the shivers coming.

Jimmy reached down and picked up the fuse box cover. Inside it was less than a cup of gas. As Henry stood up, he held the air filter cover in his gloved hands, which contained another cup or so of gas.

"What do you plan on doing with this little bit, Henry?" Jimmy asked. "We gonna start a fire?"

Henry grinned as he walked to the interior of the car. "Yeah, you could say that," he said as he set the fuse box cover on the seat and then took Jimmy's from him. He poured Jimmy's gas onto the front seat, then he drew his Glock and pushed everyone away from the car.

"Stand back, I don't know what's gonna happen exactly," he said.

Everyone stepped back, and when they were far enough away, Henry looked up at the sky and mumbled a prayer of his own that his idea would work. Then, he aimed at the fuse box cover sitting on the seat, the gas still in it, and he fired one round directly at it.

The bullet went where he wanted it to and the gas was hit by the speeding round. Friction or a small spark was enough to ignite the gas and a second after he fired, the inside of the car whooshed into a glowing fireball, resembling a small funeral pyre as the fumes ignited.

"Hot damn, it worked!" Henry yelled as he turned to the others. "I don't believe it. Well, come on, come get warm before it goes out. Don't worry, there's no gas left in the tank and I drained the fuel line, too, so there's nothing left to explode."

Sue and Mary were hesitant at first, as if they expected the car to burst into a massive fireball at any moment, but as the others gathered around the flaming car within a few feet of it, they found they couldn't resist its warmth, and so scooted closer.

Henry had his gloves off and had stuck them on a small tree branch he jammed into the slush and snow near the car. Like a clothes line, the gloves soon were drying, as was his clothes as he moved as close to the flames as he dared. Steam rose from his clothes and he felt so hot he wondered if he was cooking, being steamed like a lobster, but he endured it, knowing the time to dry off was short, and the fire would fade when the seats and other burnable items inside the vehicle were used up.

Jimmy, rubbing his hands together, a big smile on his face for a change as he was glad to be warm, moved up next to Henry and said, "Hey, aren't you worried about the fire being seen by someone? Deaders see it and we'll have a shit load of 'em on us and if there're humans around then this is a beacon to our location."

Henry gave Jimmy one of his patented shrugs. "It doesn't matter, Jimmy. What does is that we need to rest and warm up." He patted his younger friend on the shoulder. "One problem at a time, pal."

Jimmy nodded, realizing Henry had a point. All the safety in the world wouldn't matter if they ended up freezing to death.

Raven had slipped away from the group and now she popped back up again. In her hands she held a rabbit, its neck now broken. As she moved into the circle, she dropped the rabbit in front of Henry, who looked at it and then her with a surprised look.

"I caught it, so you can clean it," she said flatly and then moved away to warm up by the fire.

"Sounds fair," Henry said as he pulled his panga out again and got to work, knowing time to cook it was short.

Soon, one lone rabbit was sitting on a spit a few feet from the fire, the flames licking out the open driver's door and cooking it one side at a time as Henry turned it.

Jimmy, already licking his lips, was rubbing his hands in expectation.

Ten minutes later, as the flames began to recede; the six companions shared the single rabbit. It was burnt in some places and still rare in others, as was the case with an uneven open flame, but it tasted fantastic.

Though it was hardly enough to fulfill them, it did quiet their hunger pains for a small time, and with more snow eaten to fill their empty bellies, for just a little while, they were relatively fed and warm.

When the fire died down to nothing but embers and there was no longer enough heat to stay warm, the six companions set off once more.

Though their hunger was still there and exhaustion was prevalent, for the moment, they were in high spirits. Their boots had been dried in the fire, though Jimmy's were a little singed when he had put them too close to the flames, and each of them was now relatively warm and dry.

After an hour of leaving the burnt car behind, the cold set in once more and the warmth of the blaze was just a memory.

Plodding through the forest, they continued onward, single file the easiest way to traverse the path Henry had found. Signs of life were spotted, spores from deer and coyote.

Henry was on point, with Mary, behind him, followed by Sue, Raven, Cindy and then Jimmy, who was the rear guard.

Three hours of continuous walking later, and everyone on the verge of collapse, Henry came out of a dense tree line to find he was on the remains of an old road.

The pavement was cracking and flaking away on the edges and there was just the hint of a white double line still visible running down its middle.

The road led two ways. Higher up into the mountains, or downward to parts unknown. Given their state of exhaustion, downward was the direction Henry chose, the others all agreeing completely.

As they marched side by side in pairs of two, Jimmy kept turning around. He had the feeling he was being watched, but each time he turned, there was nothing there.

"You okay?" Henry asked him one time when he saw his friend spin around abruptly.

"Yeah, I just…I think we're being watched."

Henry nodded. "Yeah, I have that feeling, too, but then I caught a look at what it was."

Jimmy gripped his shotgun tighter as he began to flick his eyes back and forth. "Shit, really? So what's the plan? When do we double-back and get them?"

Henry smiled as he shook his head. "There's not a *them* to get, Jimmy. It's one deader. It's off to our right and for some reason it hasn't come out of the brush." He gestured to the right, at the edge of the tree line, and nodded to a large patch of shrubs they were passing, most of the branches flattened by the heavy snow.

"Look past those bushes and you can see it. It's a sorry specimen if I ever saw one. The only reason I haven't taken it out is it's not worth the trouble."

Jimmy flicked his gaze to where Henry was gesturing, and sure enough, he soon spotted a lone ghoul staggering through the snow. From where he was on the road, Jimmy thought the ghoul looked like a lost child in the woods and he could see why Henry wasn't bothering with it.

"So what? We just let it follow us?"

Henry nodded. "Yeah, if it comes too close we can deal with it, otherwise, leave it be." He turned to look Jimmy in the eyes. "We've been through this before, Jimmy. We can't kill all of 'em, so we need to have some restraint."

Jimmy's face took on a serious look and his voice grew low as he said, "That's your rule, Henry, not mine. If I have my way, then every damn one of those fuckers will be put down by my hand sooner or later."

Henry raised his left hand, his index finger pointed at Jimmy. "And I respect that, just as long as your plan doesn't endanger the rest of us."

"Understood," he replied. "Then you have no complaint if I wanna take care of that bastard?"

Henry looked at Mary and Sue who were walking together. They had both heard the conversation, but were staying out of it. Henry turned back to Jimmy. "It's your choice, Jimmy. If you want to expend the energy to take down one lone deader then knock yourself out."

Jimmy grinned widely. "Can I borrow your panga?"

"Sure, he ya go," Henry said and pulled it from its sheath and handed it to him hilt first. "But make sure you clean it before you give it back."

"Done," Jimmy smiled, turned to look at Cindy, pointed to the forest, and said, "I'm gonna get me a dead one." Then he jogged off the road and into the brush as the others watched him go.

Cindy moved up next to Henry, with Mary and Sue already gathered close to him, but Henry hadn't stopped walking to wait for Jimmy to deal with the zombie.

"Aren't we going to wait for him?" Cindy asked as she began walking backwards so she could keep Jimmy in sight.

Henry shook his head no. "If he wants to do this, then he can, but I'm not gonna stop and wait. I told him it was a waste of time. I'm not his father."

"But you're the leader of us, aren't you?" Mary interjected.

Henry glanced over his shoulder to Mary; he shrugged. "If I'm the leader then he would've done what I said. So there's your answer, I guess. Now, I'm gonna keep going, you can stay and wait or come with me."

Cindy stopped walking and crossed her arms over her chest. "Well, if there's a choice, I'll wait for Jimmy, in case he needs some help."

Mary and Sue looked at Henry, then at Jimmy's back as he stomped through the snow and then back to each other.

"Henry's right, Cindy," Mary said. "Jimmy was asked to leave it alone and he didn't. You stay and watch his back, the rest of us are going to keep walking. Catch up when he's done."

Cindy looked to Raven as the girl walked past her. "Raven, are you going, too?"

Raven shrugged. "Waste of time, it's not bothering us, not worth the risk. I'll keep going, too."

"Fine, then go, we'll catch up," Cindy said.

Henry was ten feet away and still walking. But he stopped and turned around. "Hey, Cindy, watch his back good, you know how he gets."

Cindy's visage softened at his words and she nodded. "It wouldn't be the first time I had to save his ass," she said with a grin.

"Okay," Henry said. "If you take too long we'll see about taking a break down the road if we can find a good place to stop, give you a chance to catch up. If you run into real trouble fire off a few shots and we'll come running."

"Done," she said, and began walking back the way they'd come, wanting to reach Jimmy before he did something stupid.

Henry watched her go, then he turned and continued on, his boots slapping the slush and snow, careful not to slip on the hidden ice beneath the crust of white.

He felt a pang of regret for continuing on, but if he gave in this time, then before he knew it there would be an argument about this and that and soon there would be a discussion about everything. Though they were basically a democracy, he was still the leader and any good team knew only one person could call the shots. Too many decision makers and there was no time to act, only discuss, and in the end that could get them all killed.

As Henry walked along a bend in the road, he glanced over his shoulder one last time, hoping he hadn't made a mistake by leaving Jimmy and Cindy behind, no matter how foolhardy Jimmy was being.

Jimmy climbed over the snow drift separating him from the ghoul, kicking snow out of his way as he walked.

Glancing over his shoulder, he saw the others walking away, but also saw that Cindy was staying behind. He felt a well of love growing inside for her, one even greater than before; she was watching his back.

The ghoul slowed its shamble and turned to face Jimmy. As Jimmy moved closer to it, he saw it was in very bad shape. One arm was missing, only a jagged stump exposed to the weather, and one leg looked as if it was broken. As the zombie walked, the leg dragged behind it like a lifeless tree branch, leaving marks in the snow.

Its face was the worst of all. The skin had dried into a brown, leathery parchment, the lips pulled back to expose the gums beneath. Bits of flesh, now dried, still protruded from the yellow and brown teeth, and its nose hung askew, waiting for the right moment to fall off completely.

Its eyes were sunken, pools of white, and both ears were missing.

The actual body was so emaciated the ghoul resembled a walking skeleton and as Jimmy moved to within a few feet of it, he wondered how it was able to keep moving in such a decomposed state. But then he put such trivial thoughts from his mind, raised the panga, and lunged at the ghoul, slicing its head off in one meaty *thwack*.

The head fell into the snow to disappear in a snow drift and the body toppled over to twitch for a moment and remain still.

"Too fucking easy," he muttered to himself, his breath blowing out in a thick cloud. "That's one less of you bastards in the world."

Suddenly, Cindy shouted and he glanced over his shoulder to see what she wanted, and he spotted her waving to him from the road. But now her rifle was up and she was aiming it at him and he didn't understand why, when without warning, she fired at him.

Standing perfectly still, not comprehending why on earth she would want to shoot him, he felt the bullet whine by his ear and a second later his body reacted and he dropped to the snow-covered ground.

"What the fuck, Cindy! What's going on!"

She replied by firing again and again, the bullets flying over his head like angry hornets. Though he couldn't imagine what had gotten into her, he swung his shotgun from off his shoulder and was about to bring it to bare on her, for if she was trying to kill him he had no choice, when he heard footsteps crunching behind him in the snow crusted layer covering the forest floor.

He spun around quickly, and his eyes went wide when he saw five ghouls stumbling toward him, each in different stages of decomposition. No sooner did he spot them then two of their heads exploded, the faces dissolving in a glorious spray of brown, rotting brains and skull fragments.

As gobbets of flesh splattered the pristine snow, Jimmy realized Cindy wasn't shooting at him, but at the roamers that had appeared as if by magic in the woods, exactly at his position.

As the three remaining ghouls came at him, he rolled to the right and used his shotgun to devastating effect.

One blast took a ghoul in the midsection, sheering off the upper torso from the lower half, and the ghoul tumbled over like a fallen tree. The legs kicked for a few second as intestines painted the snow a dark color that once might have been the blood.

The last two zombies Jimmy shot in the head, the shotgun blasts ripping off the heads and blowing them into a hundred bloody fragments. As the headless bodies fell forward, a dark ichor seeping from the stumps, he rolled to his knees and waved to Cindy, who returned it and lowered her rifle, seeing that the threat was over.

Jimmy stood up, and he saw another four ghouls now very dead with headshots lying a few feet away from the first group. These were the targets Cindy was shooting at and he didn't want to think what might have happened if she hadn't been there to look out for him.

Turning, he jogged back to her, cresting a snow drift to practically have her fall into his arms.

"Oh, Christ, Jimmy, I thought you were a goner for sure," she said as she hugged him.

"I might have been if not for you," he replied as he hugged her. "You saved my ass yet again, baby."

"That ass is mine, lover, and I'll be damned if any old deader is gonna bite it off." She kissed him on the lips and he felt her warmth. "If anyone's gonna bite it off, it's gonna be me."

He laughed and pushed her aside, bringing up his shotgun at the sound of footsteps coming back up the road.

Cindy spun around and leveled her M-16, the two lovers ready to send the next attackers on the last train west, when Henry, followed by the others, rounded the bend, their weapons drawn and a look of concern on their faces.

Jimmy waved that there was no cause for alarm and he and Cindy began walking to meet the others.

"What the hell was all that shooting?" Henry called as he slowed and stopped in front of Jimmy and Cindy.

"Nothing, Henry, it was nothing," Jimmy said. "It looked like that deader wasn't alone after all. When I went to put it down, a few more popped up. Cindy took care of most of 'em and I got the rest with my baby here." Jimmy patted his shotgun lovingly. He loved the way the shotgun was a room sweeper, and he didn't have to particularly aim with the weapon. Just point in the general area and let loose, and nature would take its course, by shredding whatever was in front of him.

"No kidding?" Henry asked. "See, I told you to leave it be," he said, angry. "You could have gotten yourself killed, and for what?"

"Henry, leave it, it's over," Mary said by his side as behind them, Sue and Raven were just catching up.

"No, Mary, he should have listened to me. What would have happened if he had gotten bit or worse? And for what? To take down one more deader in a world that's full of 'em." Henry turned to face Jimmy. "You were reckless and you jeopardized us all."

"Hey, old man," Jimmy snapped, "just wait a fucking minute. It's my life and if I want to risk it, that's my business."

Henry shook his head, his eyes flaring with rage, but then, he caught himself and paused, as if he was counting from one to ten to calm down a little.

"No, Jimmy, it's not your life. When we agreed to travel together then all our lives belong to each other. I thought you'd learned that by now. I guess I was wrong." He turned away and began walking. "I'm done talking to someone that doesn't want to listen. Make sure my panga is clean and give it back to me later." He joined with Sue and Raven and headed back down the road.

"Henry, wait!" Jimmy called but Mary touched his arm and shook her head. "Don't, Jimmy, just let it go for now. When he calms down later you can talk to him some more. You know how he gets. In the end, he wasn't trying to control you, he just didn't want anything to happen to you, not for such a stupid reason."

"Maybe so, Mary, but it's my reason, and if I believe it's worth it then I have a right to do what I want," Jimmy said.

She shrugged. "Maybe, but Henry has a point. If you get hurt, it would be him and the rest of us that would have to take care of you. Hell, Henry would carry you on his back until we found help if he had to. You know that. So before you go 'head and say it's your right, just think about that one." She glanced at Cindy and winked, the two women sharing a nod, then she turned and began jogging after the others, leaving Jimmy and Cindy to stand alone once more.

Jimmy scratched his cheek, as he wiped away a small piece of bone fragment from his face.

"Shit, Cindy, what do think about this? Do you take their side, too?"

She shook her head. "I'm on your side, babe, that's all that matters. As for who's right or wrong…" she shrugged. "Come on, the others are getting quite a lead on us, we better get moving, too."

She took his left arm in hers as they began walking down the road, the snow now crushed and disturbed from the companions' boots.

"That was nice shootin', babe," Jimmy commented as they walked. "Ya know, for a brief moment there, I almost thought you were shooting at me."

She chuckled at his statement and pulled him closer, hugging him. "Aw, baby, you might make me want to kill you sometimes but I would never do it. I love you too much."

He opened his mouth for a rebuttal, but then closed it again. Thinking about it for a second, he didn't really know how to reply to her statement, so he decided for once in his life to just shut up.

The two walked on in silence, and upon turning the bend in the road, they soon spotted the others, each walking in pairs once more.

They picked up their pace to catch up.

It was Sue who spotted the small light through the trees.

The drizzle had slowed to the point it was nonexistent, and with night having descended, the road was hidden, only a dim outline to separate it from the tree line.

As they traversed the road, it opened up so that one side became nothing but a steep incline. If one of them accidentally wandered off the road in the dark, there would be no way for them to rescale the hill and return to the others.

So Henry had everyone stay as close to the opposite side as possible, and even then, with no light, they would wander away from the side only to be pulled back by one of the group.

The road wound downwards, twisting and turning constantly until the companions had no idea in what direction they were heading.

And then Sue spotted the light in the midst of the trees when she accidentally wandered too close to the edge of the incline, Henry pulling her back before she could slip off. At first she assumed it was a reflection, perhaps of some moonlight that had cut through the cloud cover, but then, as she continued walking, she saw it again and again. No matter where she moved, the light remained, and she finally told the others of her discovery.

"Could be trouble," Mary suggested as she looked out into the woods at the light, the others by her side.

Henry grunted an ascent. "True, but it's not like we have a lot of options here, people. We need shelter and food and that's our best chance at finding it."

"So, what?" Jimmy asked. "We just go over there and hope for the best?"

Henry shook his head, and then realizing Jimmy could see him, he said, "No, Jimmy. When we get closer, you all stay behind and I'll go find out what I can. If we all go to that light in the dark, we could end up blundering in on some cannie camp or who the hell knows what else. I'll go alone, and if it's safe, I'll signal for you to follow."

"What kind of a signal?" Cindy asked.

Henry gave it a quick thought and said, "I'll have whoever's out there douse the light. If it goes out for a few seconds and then comes back on, that means it's safe to follow me."

"And what if the light doesn't go out?" Sue asked with concern.

Henry didn't hesitate this time. "Then I'm dead, and you should move on, and try to find what I had no luck in finding …someplace safe."

"Oh, Henry," Sue said, but he stopped her.

"That's how it is, Sue, you know that. There's no use talking about it." He looked at the outlines of each of the group in the dark. "So, are we all onboard with this?"

No one disagreed, as it was the most prudent way to find out if it was safe. Better they lose one member than all of them.

"Yeah, Henry," Jimmy said. "But I've got one thing to say."

"Go 'head."

"If that light doesn't go out, and that means your dead, I know those bastards are gonna pay…in blood."

Henry reached out and touched Jimmy's shoulder so his friend would know he was reaching for him, then he lowered his hand so the two could shake. "Jimmy, I wouldn't have it any other way."

Henry made his way down a well used path, now covered in snow, and paused for a moment to glance over his shoulder. He could just make out the small glade where his friends were waiting for him.

Turning back around, he continued walking.

When he came to the light Sue had spotted from the road a few minutes later, he saw it was an oil lantern, hanging from a black, steel post.

The lantern signified the beginnings of a gravel driveway, most of it cleared of snow so a person could walk easily.

The driveway was lined on both sides with rhododendrons, their leaves dripping wet and in the darkness resembling green, protruding tongues with mouths hidden just behind them. Henry had the feeling he was walking into the lair of a giant monster, those mouths just waiting to devour him alive.

Though the bushes seemed to press in on him, he shrugged off his wild imagination, and continued walking up the driveway, his boots crunching on the crushed gravel.

The driveway was long, and as he followed it, he began catching glimpses though the gaps in the bushes and trees of a building, its framework made of stone and iron.

As he rounded a tight corner, he found himself looking up at a grand old house, two stories with ornate architecture, a pitched roof, a heavy wooden front door, and a foundation made of concrete blocks.

Though heavy curtains were drawn over the first floor windows, light seeped through the cracks, and when Henry turned around to look behind him, he saw nothing but wilderness. The house was tucked away so far into the woods that it couldn't be detected unless someone knew exactly where to search for it, which made him wonder why the occupants would want to have a light on a post advertising there location.

Looking up, silhouetted against the dark sky, he saw the brick chimney, and smoke rising from it, indicating a fire was going somewhere in the house. Just thinking about sitting in front of a roaring fire had Henry sighing with pleasure.

As he stood in the driveway, admiring the home and wondering who could be living inside it, the subtlest hint of music floated on the air, and as he listened more intently, he heard the distinctive sound of a piano playing.

He realized standing there would get him nothing, so with a deep breath, he walked up to the ornate porch with ten stone steps, climbed them, and stood in front of the large main door. It was made of oak or some other heavy wood, varnished with a dark stain, and there was a bronze doorknocker set at head height in the shape of an eagle, the round ring to use for knocking hanging out of the bird's beak.

He checked his Glock to make sure it was where it was supposed to be, then let his hand drop down to his panga. If there was trouble, he could only pray he would have time to draw his weapons.

He reached out and knocked three times, as if he was a salesman dropping by to see if the homeowner wanted to buy the latest vacuum cleaner, knife set or encyclopedia collection.

Then, he waited.

Immediately, the music stopped from inside the house and Henry heard nothing but silence.

He waited for almost a full minute, wondering what he should do next. Should he knock again? That seemed pointless as the homeowner obviously knew he was on the porch, or should he just leave, deciding it was all a mistake.

But when he felt how cold he was as well as knowing how bad off the others were, he knew that wasn't really an option.

It was while he wrestled with what to do next that he heard the door click as someone began to unlock it. It took a while, as the locks were many, and it didn't surprise Henry at all. This secluded in the forest, good locks would have been a necessity even before the world fell apart.

It was as he waited for the locks to stop clicking that the door was suddenly thrown open, and before he could so much as reach for his Glock, he found himself staring down the muzzle of a very large shotgun.

"You so much as move a muscle and you're dead," a voice said from within the shadows of the house.

Henry thought that was an excellent idea.

"Shit, it's been almost a half hour and the light still hasn't gone out," Jimmy said worriedly. "Something's happened to Henry, I just know it."

The five companions were standing around, cold and impatient as they waited for the signal from Henry that it was safe to approach whatever lay beyond the light.

"Relax, Jimmy," Mary said softly, calmly. "He's fine; we need to give him time. Whoever he meets, he's going to have to explain carefully that there are five more armed people in the woods. If he doesn't do it right, whoever's out there might think we're raiders, or worse."

"I don't know, Mary, maybe Jimmy's right," Cindy said. "It has been a while and if something's happened and all we did was sit here and wait..."

Mary shook her head. "No, we wait here like Henry said."

"But I'm freezing my ass off out here," Jimmy said as he slapped his gloved hands together."

"We all are, Jimmy," Sue added, sitting next to Raven on a fallen tree, as the teenage girl passed the time by honing her fingernails with a nail file. A few needed tending to after the fight with the zombies.

Sue happened to glance toward the light, and when she did, she saw it blink out. "Hey, the light's gone out."

All eyes went to the light far off in the woods and each waited, praying this was the signal from Henry. Mary was counting softly, her lips moving, and when she reached ten seconds, the light came back on.

"That's it, that's the signal, thank God he's okay," Mary said as she let out the breath she was holding.

Jimmy went to the front of the group and jumped up and down like a kid going to the circus. "So, come on, let's go already, what the hell are you all waiting for? Man, I can't wait to get warm."

"What makes you think there's a place there to get warm?" Cindy asked.

"Wishful thinking, babe, wishful thinking."

Cindy and Mary looked at one another in the gloom of the forest and both smiled at each other. "Think it's safe?" Cindy asked her.

Mary shrugged, a gesture she'd picked up from Henry. "Guess it has to be or else Henry would never have signaled us?"

"That's true," Cindy added, and with Sue and Raven by her and Mary's side, they headed off in the direction of the light, not knowing what was there, but knowing if Henry had signaled them, it must be safe.

Fifteen minutes earlier.

Henry swallowed the knot in his throat as he stared down the muzzle of the shotgun, a wisp of gray hair appearing out of the shadows behind the weapon.

"Who are you? What do you want?" a voice asked, and Henry immediately knew it was a woman, old if he was correct.

"My…" Henry began and then cleared his throat as he regained some of his composure. From his experience in the new world, he was fairly certain if the old woman had wanted him dead, then she would have fired upon opening the door.

"My name's Henry Watson. I'm a traveler. I saw your light at the end of the driveway and I was hoping you could spare some food, maybe a warm place to sleep for the night. My friends and I…"

"What friends?" the woman demanded. "Where are they?"

Henry decided all or nothing was what was needed here and he went for the former, so he continued. "My friends are waiting for me to signal them if it's safe to come here. We didn't know what was here and didn't want to arrive in a group." He tried to smile, despite the shotgun in his face. "Thought it would be better if I just came alone first and said hello."

The old woman leveled the shotgun for another moment and then abruptly lowered it. As she stepped closer to him, he could see her smiling.

"Why didn't you say so, dear. There always room for hungry mouths at my dinner table. We love guests. You'll have to forgive me, I thought you might have been from town."

"Town?" he asked, curious.

"Yes, dear. About twelve miles from here." She waved it away as if it meant nothing. "It doesn't matter, what does is that you're cold and hungry. Where are my manners? You go get your friends and have them come back; I'll put a pot of tea on while I'm waiting for your return."

Henry nodded. "Thank you, that's mighty generous of you. I'll be back in a few minutes."

"Take your time, dear, we'll be here."

He paused that time at her use of the term we. If there had been others in the house, he would have expected them to have shown themselves at the sound of him knocking. Deciding the old woman must be a little off, he ignored the term, and with a wave, went to signal the others that it was safe to come to the house.

Her name was Abigail Yorkshire and she was seventy-two years old. Her silver hair was done up in a bun and her cheeks were red, like small apples, her kind eyes always seeming to be looking at you when you looked the other way. She had a wide smile, too perfect, and Henry assumed they were dentures.

She wore a flowing black dress and a large silver necklace. On the end of it was a locket in which she told the companions there was a picture of her and her husband, Philmore. That was the we she referred to, her husband, who she said was always with her and thus why she referred to herself as *we*.

After washing up in simple basins of water taken from an underground well located at the rear of the house, the six companions were now sitting in the dining room of the old house, each waiting for Abigail to return with the main course of the meal she had offered them before they would retire to their bedrooms for the night. She had told them that the house was quite large and there was plenty of room for everyone.

All of the companions felt as if they had hit the lottery, back when such things still existed.

The meal had started out with a hearty salad of home grown lettuce, complete with ripe cherry tomatoes. Abigail had a greenhouse and grew her own vegetables. The dressing was a simple oil and vinegar, taken from the large pantry stockpiled with flour, sugar and other canned necessities for survival.

All eyes looked up when Abigail wheeled in a table, and on it was large steel tureen filled more than halfway with a rich stew. More vegetables were in ceramic side dishes; carrots, green beans and onions.

To the companions, after traveling for so long and only having their meager rations, it was a feast fit for a king and they dug in happily the instant Abigail ladled out a bowl full.

"Please, eat all you want, my friends. I imagine after your journey through the mountains you must be famished. There's plenty for all, so don't be shy."

"No worries, there, ma'am," Jimmy said and dove in, shoveling spoonful after spoonful into his mouth. It was so hot he burned his tongue but he didn't care, so pleased to be eating real food. The gravy was a dark brown with bits of flour still in it, reminding him of a homemade stew his mother used to make. Jimmy finished off his first bowl and quickly asked for more, receiving it without question.

"So, Abigail," Henry began as he swallowed a mouthful of stew. The spices were so strong he could barely taste the meat, but it was still hot and good, filling his stomach so he was already content after only a few mouthfuls. "How do you manage out here all alone? Especially with all the snow."

Abigail smiled at Henry and her eyes filled with sweetness. "Oh, my, Henry, that's so kind of you to ask, but this old house is made of stern stock. We've managed just fine out here."

Mary spoke up. "You do know what's happened out in the rest of the world, don't you?"

Abigail nodded, her smile vanishing as sadness filled her eyes. "Oh, my dear, of course I do. We have television and radio, well, we did before they stopped working. We've even seen a few of those dead people now and then. They wander in from the mountains. I suppose it's just luck that has them finding this house, but they're easy to put down." She shook her head. "It's so horrible, but we've learned to adapt to our new world, each in his own way, am I right?" She looked to Henry with her question.

"Yes, ma'am, I would have to agree with you on that one," Henry replied.

Jimmy finished off his second helping and picked up his bowl. "Can I have some more, please?"

"Jimmy, don't be a pig," Cindy said next to him. She was eating only some of the stew, not finding the spices to her liking, the vegetable side dishes were more her preferred taste. After eating some of the stew, the spices disagreed with her to the point she had only eaten a little, finding after all this time to not have much of an appetite.

"Oh, no, dear," Abigail said, "it's perfectly fine, as I said, there's plenty for all." She stood up from her seat at the head of the table and ladled Jimmy another heaping bowl full.

"It is good," Sue said as she took a bite. "Do you grow the spices as well?"

"Yes, dear, but some are dried, I will have to admit."

"Oh, of course," Sue added and continued eating. As she finished her bowl, she suddenly felt exhausted and Henry noticed this.

"Are you all right, Sue?" he asked.

She wiped her brow with her cloth napkin. "Yes, I'm fine, I just...I guess now that we finally have a safe place to rest and with food in me, I think it's all catching up to me."

Henry nodded. "You know, now that you mention it, I am feeling wiped out."

"Me, too," Raven said simply.

"Yeah, I could go for a nap right about now," Jimmy said and in fact his eyes looked as if he could barely keep them open.

Abigail glanced at Cindy and saw she hadn't eaten very much and said, "My dear, what's the matter, don't you like my cooking?"

"Huh? Oh, yes, it's fine, it's just...I'm not a fan of some of the spices and herbs you put in the stew. I don't think they're sitting too well with me."

For just a moment, Abigail's sweet look vanished, but then it quickly reappeared.

"Oh, well, I put ginger, fennel, some lemon balm, a pinch of oregano and basil to name a few. Perhaps some of the dried spices had gotten too old. They say that can happen." She stared at Cindy, as if her *will* alone could make her eat.

Cindy, feeling uncomfortable by the old woman's glare, picked up her spoon and took a small bite. She licked her lips and smiled, nodding her head as she went in for another spoonful.

Abigail, seeing Cindy was now eating, looked away and began talking to Henry once more.

Cindy saw that Jimmy was about done with his third bowl of stew so she quickly reached out and switched bowls with him. "Here, lover, you can have mine, too."

"Oh, thanks, babe, I was just gonna ask for more." He dug in, barely slowing down to chew. She shook her head at seeing him eat like a ten-year-old, his mouth and chin covered with gravy. She handed him a cloth napkin and told him to wipe his face.

"Shit, Cindy, lighten' up, enjoy the grub," he said as he finished off her bowl. With four bowls of stew in him, he finally felt full and he burped, a quick, "excuse me," following it.

"That's our Jimmy, always a gentleman," Mary said, the others chuckling.

"Ha, ha, Mary, you're hilarious," Jimmy said and looked to Abigail. "Man, that was awesome stew, what kind of meat was that? It tasted like pork but it was hard to tell with all the spices."

Abigail nodded. "You're right on the first try, my boy. We have a few pigs out back and we kill one now and then for the meat."

"Well, it was awesome," Jimmy replied and stretched. "Man, I'm ready to go to sleep," he yawned, setting off a domino effect as each of the others then yawned. "I could go to bed right now."

"I was hoping we could all adjourn to the sitting room and have a nightcap. I have a bottle of brandy I've been itching to crack open," Abigail suggested.

Stifling a yawn, Henry nodded, then looked at each of the others, seeing the same weariness in their faces that he felt in his own. "Okay, that would be fine, but I don't think any of us could go past that. Your cooking is just too good, Abigail."

She waved his compliment away. "Oh, please, it's passable at best." She stood up and led them into a sitting room after walking down a short hallway.

A fireplace was in the corner and behind the metal grating, a fire roared, filling the room with warmth. The walls were adorned with oil paintings and a rich, plush sofa lined another wall. Two more arm chairs completed the furniture and there was more than enough room for everyone. A small end table was in the corner, and Cindy went to it and looked at the framed photos set out on top of it. She saw Abigail in them and another person, a man.

"Is this your husband?" Cindy asked as she picked up one of the photos and studied it. The man in the picture was tall, over six feet, and he had a receding hairline and smile wrinkles around his mouth. He looked happy, they both did.

Abigail went to her and took the frame back, then set it back down in the same exact spot. "Yes, dear, that's my Philmore."

Abigail went to a waist high cabinet with bottles of liquor lined up on top of it, and picked one of the glass bottles, then opened the cabinet and took out seven glasses. The glasses were made of Waterford crystal. They were thin to the point they looked like if they were squeezed too hard by a hand, they would shatter.

She opened the bottle and poured an inch of gold liquid into each glass, then, with the glasses on a silver tray, she walked the room, each of the companions taking one.

"To your health," Abigail said as she raised her glass and each of the companions did the same. As she drank hers, the others did also, and soon a growing warmth filled their insides.

The alcohol went right to Henry's head, despite his full stomach. "Wow, that's strong, either that or I've become a lightweight," he said, his words slurred slightly.

"Ha, probably both," Jimmy said and smacked his lips.

Mary shook her head to clear it, the fogginess closing in. God she was tired. "Henry," she said. "I can't keep my eyes open anymore and I think the brandy was about it for me. I need to go lay down."

"Me, too," Sue added. "I didn't realize how truly tired I was until after eating."

"Yeah, I have to agree with you guys," Henry said.

Raven nodded as did Cindy.

Abigail set her empty glass down, picked up the silver tray, and collected everyone's glasses. An oil lamp sat on a nearby table and she picked it up, then moved to the wide archway leading back out to the hallway.

"Where are my manners. I'm so sorry. Of course you're all exhausted. I've just been so starved for company here that I'm being selfish. Truth be told, I also retire early as there isn't much to do after the sun goes down but read, and I try to save the fuel for the fires and there are only so many candles. Come, come, I'll show you to your rooms and in the morning, we can talk some more."

On unsteady legs, each of the companions rose from their seats and followed Abigail down a long hallway to a large, sweeping staircase leading to the second floor.

"Feel free to take any of the rooms upstairs with the exception of the very last room. That's mine," she said. "There is also a bathroom upstairs but of course there's no running water. A bucket in the tub can be used to flush, but only if absolutely necessary. We all have to rough it now, I'm afraid." She was on the first step, looking at each of the companions now gathered in a group. "Oh, by the way, would you like to leave your weapons with me for safe-keeping? I could store them until tomorrow, that way there won't be any accidents in the middle of the night." She eyed Henry's panga. "That is a handsome knife you have there, Henry. What is that, a machete?"

"Panga, and thank you, but we'd prefer to hold onto our weapons."

Abigail's face seemed to grow hard as if storm clouds had rolled in on a clear morning, but it was for less than a second, a smile quickly appearing like a summer's day. "Of course, of course, it was just an idea, don't worry about it. Well, off you go to your beds. There are twin beds and full ones depending on what room you take."

"We'll figure it out, thank you, Abigail. You've been very kind," Mary added as she yawned, covering her hand with her mouth. "Oh, wow, I can't stop yawning," she said as she saw Jimmy and Cindy doing the same after seeing her.

Henry nodded. "Tell me about it, I can barely keep my eyes open."

Abigail turned and walked down the stairs past Henry and the others. "Then go on, and sleep tight. I have a few things to clean up from dinner before I retire. It's not often we have so many guests staying here. I have to tell you this is quite a treat."

"We're just glad we found you," Henry said as he began to climb the stairs with Sue on his arm. "Goodnight."

"Goodnight, dear, sleep tight, all of you."

The companions climbed the stairs, Jimmy barely able to put one foot in front of the other, he was so tired. Cindy helped him along. She was tired too but not as much as the others seemed to be. She didn't give it much thought as she reached the landing and pointed to a door. "Me and Jimmy will take that one, Henry. If I have to carry him another three feet he's gonna fall over."

"Fine, Cindy, go 'head. Me and Sue will take that one and Raven and Mary can have the one next to us."

"Sounds good," Mary said and walked past him to the indicated door, swaying a little as if drunk with Raven by her side. Both went in without another word, the door clinking softly once more.

"Henry," Cindy called. "Are we gonna have someone on watch tonight?"

Henry yawned loudly, and shook his head to fight off the grogginess suffusing his body. "Nah, Cindy, we should be safe enough here. If Abigail wanted to do us harm, there's been ample opportunity, don't you think?"

"Yeah, I guess so, okay, I need to get Jimmy to bed." She opened her door and shoved Jimmy inside, then with a wave, she was in and closed the door.

Henry did the same, and soon he was closing the door to his room and looking at Sue.

"I hope you don't mind if I don't want to wash up some more before bed, Sue," Henry said as he stepped into the bedroom. A full-size bed greeted him, and it was as if it was screaming at him to fall into it.

She shook her head. "No, not tonight, you can skip it," she replied "I don't think I have the energy to wash up either." She was sitting in a chair near the window, bent over as she took off her boots, and she realized Henry hadn't replied to her. "Henry? Did you hear me? I said it's..." she stopped short and grinned widely. Henry was lying face down on the bed, his eyes closed, his mouth hanging open, sleeping soundly.

She went to him, took off his boots and took a spare blanket from a side chair, then after covering him up, she climbed into bed. She kissed him once on the cheek, the man not so much as stirring. Then she stretched out and closed her eyes.

She was out in seconds.

Cindy carried Jimmy across the bedroom and dropped him on the first twin bed. His body fell half on, half off, but he didn't stir; he was already sleeping. She went to him, wanting to get him on the bed better. As it was now, only his upper half was on the bed, his knees on the floor. For all purposes, he looked like a small boy praying at the side of his bed; only he had decided to rest his head.

She tried once but he was just dead weight and finally she gave up. Pulling the blanket off the bed, she draped it around him.

"Good enough," she breathed heavily as she kicked off her boots and went to the other bed.

Stretching out, she closed her eyes, but though she was exhausted, sleep wouldn't come. Her mouth was bone dry and she began to feel a headache, the steady throbbing just behind her eyes.

Jimmy began to snore and she let out a large sigh, not understanding why she couldn't fall asleep. She was definitely tired enough, she knew that, and by the way the others had looked, she figured they were probably all fast asleep by now, just like Jimmy.

She lay silently, her hands on her stomach, her headache pounding for almost a half hour when she began to hear an odd noise floating in from somewhere in the house.

It was a sound she couldn't put her finger on. A *thunk* sound.

At first she ignored it, as it wasn't her problem. Maybe Abigail was working in the kitchen?

But then she felt pressure on her bladder and realized she needed to pee.

But exhausted as she was, she still tried to ignore all the distractions and squeezed her eyes tighter, as if she could make sleep come.

The *thunk* sound repeated itself, steady, like a heartbeat every minute or so.

Cindy sat up, another heavy sigh escaping her lips. Between the thunks, Jimmy's snoring, her headache, and the need to pee, she knew there was no way she would be sleeping any time soon. Plus, she had a feeling she was now overtired, and that all she would be doing is wasting time if she didn't want to admit it to herself.

Figuring the bathroom should be first, she slid out of bed and padded to the door. She glanced at her boots, lying like two dead carcasses in the gloom at the foot of the bed, but decided to leave them. It wasn't like she was going outside, just to the end of the hallway.

With a brief look at Jimmy, she saw he was sleeping heavily, a thin line of drool now collecting under his mouth and saturating the sheet, and she opened the door and stepped into the hallway.

The hardwood was cold on her feet and she felt a chill go up her spine from the soles of her feet.

In the gloom of the hallway, she quietly walked to the bathroom, did her business and then returned to her bedroom door.

She was about to go inside when she heard the thunk sound again.

Her curiosity getting the better of her, she padded to the stairs and went down them, careful to stay on the outer edges of each step so as to avoid any creaking steps. She needn't have feared this, as the stairs were made from old world craftsmanship and were solid as the day they were built.

Walking through the house, she ended up in the back, and found a door cracked a few inches. As she studied the door, to her it looked like the door was supposed to be closed, because a cold breeze was blowing into the house through the opening. Peering into the doorway, she saw a set of stairs leading down to what had to be the basement, the darkness all but complete, a dull glow coming from somewhere at the bottom.

Another *thunk* sound came to her and Cindy bit her lip, wondering if she should go get Henry.

Whoever was down there had left the door open by accident and the noise of their work was filtering into the house. As she felt the edge of the door, she saw it was heavy, and if it had been closed, the noise would not have reached her upstairs.

This was a mystery and Cindy was a curious woman.

Deciding she would check out whatever was going on and if it was somehow serious, she would go get Henry, she began walking down the stairs. The third one down creaked and she paused, hoping she hadn't been heard, and when the *thunk* came to her again, she knew she was fine.

She continued downward.

At the bottom of the stairs she found herself in the basement, just as she'd figured and her eyes took in all the odds and ends. A small oil lantern hung on the far wall, lit but turned down low, and it gave off just enough light to see her surroundings easily.

Her eyes played over old boxes, a small workbench with tools, and other miscellaneous items one would expect to find in a cellar.

The thunk noise came to her again and she turned her head to the right, seeing the outline of an outer door.

Her feet were cold on the concrete floor but she ignored it, wanting to know what that damn noise was. There was a hammer on the workbench and she picked it up, wanting to have something as a weapon out of habit. She had seen too much in the past two years to travel unarmed, and regretted not taking her sidearm with her. Even her knife would have been better than nothing.

Reaching the door, she opened it slowly, the cold frigid air flowing over her and causing her to get the chills. She might have closed the door right then, not wanting to freeze, but the thunk sound came to her and prodded her onward.

There was a pair of old rubber boots at the foot of the two stairs leading to the door and she borrowed them, sliding them on. They were three sizes too big but they did the job of keeping her feet dry as she stepped out into a snow laden path.

As she closed the door behind her, careful not to accidentally lock herself out, she saw a small building about twenty feet away.

The window facing her in the building had a ragged curtain over it, but light still spilled through the cracks. The thunk came again, and she began walking down the path, her rubber boots crunching on ice crystals from where the snow had melted to then freeze over. She wished she had a jacket on but she knew she would only be a few minutes, so she gritted her teeth and walked up to the small building.

Reaching the window, she looked inside, not knowing what to expect, but as she rubbed some of the condensation from the glass and peered inside, her eyes went wide in shock at the tableau before her and everything she'd seen and heard that night at dinner came into focus.

Bending over, she promptly threw up, splashing the rubber boots with her dinner.

Cindy wiped her mouth, feeling better after vomiting.

She didn't know why, but she felt slightly better, less groggy than before.

Peering back into the building, she let her eyes take in the charnel house one more time.

There were three people inside. Two were male, and the older man she recognized from the photos; Abigail had said it was her husband, Philmore. So he wasn't dead.

The other man was at least thirty years younger, and by the family resemblance, Cindy knew the younger man had to be Philmore and Abigail's son. Abigail was also inside. She was working at a counter in the corner, chopping pink meat into cubes and setting them into a pan.

But that wasn't what had Cindy vomiting.

What had shocked her was what Philmore was doing. The man was standing in the center of a room at a large square table with his son beside him. The older man had a large cleaver in his right hand, and each time he brought it down, Cindy heard the thunk that had floated to her as she lay in bed.

The sound was what happened each time the cleaver chopped into the human torso lying on the table, the cleaver slicing through meat and bone to strike the table.

Male or female, she couldn't tell the gender of the torso, but it was definitely human. The arms were gone and the insides had been taken out, much like the cavity of a cleaned chicken, and Philmore was hard at work cutting up the rib cage into decent sized ribs. At the end of the table were the arms and legs of the torso, the meat waiting for its turn to be chopped up by Abigail.

From Cindy's perspective, it looked like the father was teaching the son the family business, the son nodding as the father made certain cuts, like a butcher teaching his son his trade.

Stumbling back in horror, Cindy now understood why the stew had tasted *off*. It wasn't spices that had made her dislike it, but something far, far worse. And now that she was feeling better, she had a feeling she knew why she had been so tired, but not as tired as the rest of her friends.

She hadn't partaken of the stew, only having eaten a few bites to be polite while the others had all eaten heartily, Jimmy the most with four servings.

The stew had been drugged, and the painful truth was obvious after seeing the torso being cut up.

The companions had been drugged so they would be easy pickings, so Abigail and her family could slaughter them in their sleep, thus having more meat to cut up and feed to the next unknowing travelers and so continue the cycle.

And then she saw movement in the corner of the building and her eyes went wide when she saw it was a zombie.

It was tied to the wall by its waist, the reason being it had no arms. Cindy watched as Abigail walked over to the ghoul, and with an axe, hacked off one of its legs. The ghoul fell to the floor to flail about and Abigail took the leg back to the counter and began chopping it up. Cindy could see where the other flesh had been pink, the zombies flesh was dark brown, and some portions had patches of rot on them. Abigail began trimming this away to toss into a discard bucket.

Abigail turned to her husband and said, "The outlanders should be asleep by now, are we going to kill them soon?"

Philmore nodded as he chopped off another piece of the torso. "We will, I just want to finish with this one first. With six more bodies it's going to be a long night. So I want to finish with what we have before we start on the new meat."

"I get to have two of the women before we kill them, though, right, Dad?" the younger man asked.

Philmore nodded. "I told you yes, you can take two of 'em, and have some fun, but only for a few days, then they need to be processed and packed away."

The younger man grinned. "That'll be more than enough time," he said with a lecherous grin. "The hard part is deciding which ones to keep for a while."

Backing away from the window, Cindy knew she needed to get back inside and wake the others, warn them of what was going on and what was soon to happen.

As she took a step away from the building, her eyes caught a flash of white where there should be only darkness.

Something told her she needed to investigate before returning to the others, so she quickly left the path and walked to the end of the building. Here, she found a wooden cart with a tarp over it. The wind blew the edge of the tarp where it had come undone, and when it was raised slightly, Cindy saw what had attracted her attention.

Pulling the tarp back and letting it fall to the snowy ground, she saw the clean white of bones picked clean.

And human skulls, more than two dozen, if not more.

She didn't have time to count, but there were enough bones to build a lot of skeletons.

The moonlight cast a pale light on the mound of dead souls and she saw not all the bones were clean. Many still had dried flesh and meat stuck to them and though it was cold, maggots still writhed about, feeding on the rotting meat.

Cindy felt a slight warmth when she had pulled the tarp off the charnel mound and she realized the decaying meat would build up heat. With it covered, it was warm enough for the maggots to prosper, though she doubted they would live long as the temperature continued to drop.

Still, the entire fetid pile crawled with white worms, sliding between open jaws and gaping eyes sockets.

The worst thing she found was that the bones on top of the pile, the ones that had just been added, looked very fresh, no rot had touched them yet and she felt another bout of revulsion fill her as she tasted bile at the back of her throat once more. With an iron will, she forced it down.

Fighting off a wave of nausea at what she and her friends had eaten unwillingly, she turned away to return to them, all the while visualizing the large pot filled with stew, the greasy meat swimming in the dark gravy, and seeing Jimmy eating bite after bite as the gravy coated his lips and ran down his chin.

"Henry, get up, damn it," Cindy whispered into his ear as she tried to wake him up.

He groaned and rolled over, then began snoring. Sue was out as well and hadn't stirred when Cindy entered the bedroom.

After discovering the bones, Cindy had crept back to the basement, slid off the boots, wanting to put them back where she'd found them so as not to be discovered, and had then taken the steps to the first floor as fast as she could. Once inside the house, she ignored stealth, knowing the only people who posed a threat were still outside.

She ran up the wide stairs to the second floor and right to Henry's bedroom door. Slipping in, she dropped to the side of the bed and began shaking him, but no matter how much she pulled and shook him, he refused to wake up.

She knew it was the drugged food that had him sleeping heavier than usual and she also knew that if she had eaten the stew like the rest of them, she would be asleep too, all of them easy game to the twisted family living in the house.

Now it was up to her to save them all or else they would be next in the stew pot.

She idly wondered if she should take the family on by herself, simply get her M-16, go back to the building they were in, and blow them all to hell, but she decided recklessness might not work.

For all she knew, they had guns, and if she was caught off guard, as she didn't know the entire layout of the house, she might end up getting shot or worse before she knew it had happened.

Or worse, she went to deal with the threat while the threat came for her friends. She could end up in an empty building while her friends were slaughtered in their sleep.

No, she needed to watch over them, and if the murderous family came for her friends, she would deal with them.

"Damn it, Henry, wake the fuck up," she hissed. Deciding she needed more drastic measures, she slapped Henry across the face. The loud crack filled the room and Henry grunted, but still he remained asleep.

She was panicking inside, though still holding it together, and she glanced around the bedroom, wondering what she could do to wake him up.

And then she saw the window and the snow piled on the outside edgework.

Coming to her feet, she went to the window, opened it, and scooped up a double-handful of snow, then took it back to Henry, and with a sigh as to what she was going to do, she pulled back the blankets and shoved the snow into Henry's shirt and pants. Then she stood back and waited.

Henry didn't move at first, but within a few seconds he began to groan, as if he was having a bad dream. His hands went to the spots the snow touched his skin and he began to rub it. Slowly at first, then more heavily.

Suddenly, his eyes snapped open and he sat up, unstable and off balance, but awake.

"Jesus, it's cold in here," he slurred as he began to twitch, the snow melting from his warm body and the cold water bringing him to a higher awareness.

His voice was groggy as he turned to see Cindy in his bedroom. "Cindy? What's wrong? What are you doing in my room? Why am I all wet and why the hell is it so damn cold in here?"

In quick, short sentences, Cindy filled him in on what she found and what she believed had happened to him and the others. When she was finished, Henry was standing and awake. His head was still full of fog, like he'd drunk way too much alcohol and it was the next morning, but with each passing second, adrenalin suffused his system, overriding the drug from the stew, his will to survive more powerful.

"Okay, we need to leave here right now." The room was spinning and he shook his head to clear it. "Look, normally I'd say we kill the cannie assholes and then leave, but I'm still pretty out of it. So we need to get everyone up and then we get the hell out of here."

"But what about Abigail and her crazy family?" Cindy asked. "They need to pay for what they've done. There were so many bones there. They've been doing this for a while."

"Maybe so," he replied and moved around the bed to rouse Sue who was still sleeping, "but it's not worth one of us getting killed. So we run. Let the next poor bastard deal with it."

"But, Henry..." she began.

He spun on her, and though he tried to snap at her, it didn't come off very forceful as he was still so groggy. "I said no, Cindy, damn it, listen to me when I give an order. Now, go get Raven and Mary, and then together we'll all get Jimmy. That damn fool ate more stew than all of us put together. He's probably so zonked out a bomb could go off and he wouldn't know it."

She looked as if she was going to protest but a hard look at Henry, in between trying to stir Sue, stopped her.

"Okay, but I don't like this one bit," Cindy said and went to the door to leave.

"Neither do I," Henry agreed and then he began gently slapping Sue on her cheeks to wake her.

Mary and Raven were easier to rouse as they hadn't eaten that much stew. Both groggy and unsteady on their feet, they listened to Cindy quickly and once they had heard the entire story, their eyes were more alert and adrenalin began to fill them.

Soon, all were up and dressed with the exception of Jimmy. Only a few minutes had passed since Cindy first woke Henry and now the five companions were in Cindy and Jimmy's room, each of them looking down on a sleeping Jimmy.

They had slapped him, poked him and sat him up, but Jimmy was still out cold, some drool sliding down his chin.

Finally, Henry had had enough of playing games and left the room, saying he would be right back.

When he returned, he carried the large bucket of water that was used in the bathroom for flushing the toilet.

With Jimmy sitting propped up on the bed, Henry walked over to him, raised the water bucket over the sleeping man's head, and poured the entire contents onto Jimmy. As the water sluiced over his head and soaked into his clothes and bed, he sputtered awake, his lips spraying water as he tried to figure out what was going on. He was about to let out a scream, but Henry placed his right hand over Jimmy's mouth, stifling him and causing him to only moan.

"Shut up, Jimmy, you'll let them know we're awake," Henry hissed as Jimmy's eyes went wide and he saw all his friends standing around him. His pupils were still dilated and he was tired, but he fought off the feeling, knowing instantly something was happening.

Henry took his hand away from Jimmy's mouth and took a step back, while Cindy handed Jimmy a towel.

"What the fuck, old man? Is this some kind of a damn joke? Why the hell would you dump a bucket of water on me?"

"Just get changed and we'll fill you in. And hurry up," Henry ordered as Cindy went to Jimmy and began unbuttoning his sodden shirt.

For a moment, Jimmy was worried when he didn't feel his .38 or see his shotgun, but Mary stepped up and showed him she was holding them. Mary had made sure to remove them and take the .38 out of its holster before Henry dumped the water on him.

Sue went to Jimmy's backpack and took out some fresh clothes, handing them to him, then once he was dressed and filled in on what was happening, he gritted his teeth and said, "Those no good fuckers, I'll kill them."

"No, you won't," Henry ordered. "Neither you or the rest of us are at peak condition. Look at you, I dumped a bucket of water on you and you can still barely stand up. Like I told the others, we leave this place and let the next bastard worry about it. I told you before, we can't save the damn world; we just need to save ourselves."

"Fine, Henry, I can't say I agree with you, but seems there's two of you in front of me, I guess I'm outnumbered," Jimmy said with a slight grin.

Henry looked at Mary and Sue who both shrugged.

"You said he's more doped up than the rest of us, he probably does see two of you," Sue said as she went to Jimmy to help him button his new shirt. "Come on, Jimmy, I'll help you."

Seconds later, Henry was at the bedroom door now and he looked over his shoulder at the others, each ready to leave.

"Okay, so no noise, we head to the front door and we leave, no stopping. Got it?"

As Henry made eye contact with each of them, they nodded in kind. "Okay, let's move."

Henry opened the bedroom door and stepped into the hallway, his Glock leading the way. Behind him, the rest of the group exited. Mary was behind Henry, followed by Raven and Sue who half-carried Jimmy between them, and Cindy took up the rear flank as she was the most alert.

Like children sneaking downstairs on Christmas morning to open presents before their parents were awake, the six warriors crept down the hallway and then to the wide stairs leading to the first floor.

"Go, I'll cover you," Henry whispered to Mary as he used the railing to steady his arm, pointing the Glock at the foyer below. "When you reach the bottom, wait for everyone to catch up."

"Okay, but pay attention," Mary said.

She climbed down the stairs one at a time, wincing with the expectation of a stair squeaking. When she made it to the bottom, she peered around the archway leading to the hallway that would take them back to the dining room, sitting room and the front door. She turned and waved to the others that it was safe.

One at a time, they each crept down the stairs, and when they were all together once more, Henry pointed to the opposite end of the hallway, to the rear of the house.

"Cindy, you take everyone out the back way. I want to gather some supplies before we head out, otherwise we're gonna be in the same shape we were in a day ago. Don't worry; I won't be taking any meat with me, no matter what it looks like."

Mary spoke up. "I'll come with you, there's no need to go alone."

He was going to say no when he saw the resolve in her eyes. "Fine, I could probably use the help, okay the rest of you, out the back way and we'll meet back where you were waiting for my signal with the light."

Cindy looked as if she was going to protest but Henry touched her on the shoulder, giving her his most sincere smile. "Hey, I'll be fine, and now I have Mary to watch my back. You guys get going, none of us are in any condition to fight right now, but we need food. And Jimmy's suffering by the look of him."

She nodded, not liking it but knowing he was right. All she had to do was look at Jimmy to see this was true. Though he had woken up initially, he was all but sleeping again. She frowned when she looked at him. Serves the idiot right for stuffing himself like a pig.

"Huh, some suffering," Raven said. "Me and Sue are the ones carrying him. He ain't light ya know."

"Try having him on top of you when we..." Cindy began but was stopped in mid-sentence.

Raven held up her hand. "Uh-uh, no thank you, that's an image I can live without."

"Okay, Henry, you and Mary be careful," Cindy said.

"Will do, now get going, our luck can't last all night," Henry replied as he winked at Sue who smiled back half-heartily.

Cindy turned and led the others to the rear of the house. Henry heard a door open and felt the cold air rush in. A second later the door clicked shut and he let out the breath he was holding. He looked to Mary and said, "Good, at least they're safe. Okay we get to the kitchen, take as much food as we can and then get the hell out of here, sound good?"

"Yes, let's do this; I want to be gone as soon as possible from this lunatic asylum." She shook her head. "I still find it hard to believe, Abigail seemed so nice. I should have known better, nothing's ever as it seems anymore."

"Tell me about it," Henry said and began walking down the hall. "Okay, stay close."

A minute later found them in the kitchen. With only the faintest amount of moonlight filtering in through the kitchen window, they could barely see, but in no time they were shoving their backpacks full of canned goods and packets of dried food. Five minutes later and they were ready to leave. It had taken longer than Henry would have liked, but there was no choice, they needed food if they were to survive in the wilderness of snow and ice.

"Okay, let's go, we've got enough," he said and Mary nodded, zipping her pack up.

Walking down the spacious hallway, Henry was beginning to feel more relaxed. The exit wasn't far and it looked like Abigail and her family was still outside in the meat shack or whatever they called it.

Perhaps it was the drugs still in his system that let Henry drop his guard more than he normally would have, but for whatever reason, he reached the end of the hallway, turned the corner that would lead to the front door, and bumped right into Abigail.

"And what do we have here?" Abigail asked as she glared at Henry and then shifted her gaze to Mary, who was standing behind him. "Were you perhaps stealing a midnight snack or were you leaving without saying goodbye? Now that's not very polite, whatever the reason you're about. Don't you know? All good meat should be in bed, waiting for the sandman to come up and slice your throats."

Henry's reflexes were slower than he would have preferred, and he only blinked at the woman in her odd clothing. For she wasn't wearing a standard dress like at dinner, now she wore a long, black rubber apron complete with rubber boots. A pair of plastic goggles covered her eyes and her gray hair was tied back into a pony tail, a shower cap on the top of her head. She looked like she was about to do some serious bloodletting and didn't want to get splattered with her victims' blood.

In her right hand, she held a wicked looking carving knife, the edge razor sharp.

"We found the footprints under the window, which one of you has been sneaking about past their bedtime, hmmm?" she asked nonchalantly. "And how in the world did you find out? It was supposed to be so simple. I drug you, you all fall asleep, and I come up and kill you one at a time. You never feel a thing. Now you've made it oh so difficult."

"Sorry to spoil your plans," Henry said.

"Indeed," Abigail replied.

As she stood perfectly still, looking at Henry, her expression remained impassive. So Henry never expected it when she brought up the carving knife, swinging it around with her right arm outstretched, the blade slicing the air and heading directly for Henry's throat.

With his nervous system impaired thanks to the drug still flowing in his blood, his reflexes were a fraction of what they might have been. Time seemed to stand still as he watched the blade coming at him.

Then something snapped inside him and he went into action, darting to the side as the knife whispered past his jugular with barely an inch of clearance. The attack put Abigail off-balance, and Henry used the opportunity to push her away from him, his Glock falling to the floor at the same time. He would have done more to keep her down for good but a bout of dizziness flooded his vision and he had to lean against the wall for support. The drug was still trying to do its job, but he was fighting off the effects with everything he had.

From behind, footsteps pounded the floor and Mary spun, holding her .38, to see Abigail's son coming at her, a long boning knife held tightly in his right hand. She never hesitated. She fired two rounds into his chest, blowing his heart apart and spraying blood onto the wall and furniture behind him as the exit wounds punched fist-sized holes out of his back. The young man was thrown back to trip over an ottoman, where he tumbled head first to the floor. His eyes were glazed over in death, dead before he landed.

Abigail saw Mary shoot her son and she let out a maniacal scream that almost had Henry clapping his hands over his ears to protect his eardrums.

"*My boy! My beautiful boy!*" she shrieked as she climbed to her feet and charged at Mary.

"Mary, look out!" Henry yelled and was about to grab Abigail and pull her back when he was stopped short and lifted six inches off the floor.

From behind him, two large hands had clasped around his neck like a vise and were now squeezing his throat. In the half-second since the hands wrapped around his neck, Henry had already begun to choke, white flashes of light dancing across his vision.

Through the haze of his faltering vision and lack of air, he saw Mary fighting with Abigail, the old woman a formidable opponent. Mary tried to shoot the old woman but her .38 was knocked from her hand by a swipe of the carving knife and Mary was now facing her hand-to-hand.

Then Henry had his own problems as he struggled to stay conscious.

"I'm going to snap your neck and suck your bones dry, little man," a low male voice growled, Henry's mouth opening and closing like a landed fish as he tried to suck in air.

For all of Henry's hardened muscles, he was like a child in the grip of the giant who had a hold of him.

Blackness was beginning to descend, and though dying, the massive adrenalin rush fueling his body was enough to override the drugs in his system and for just a moment Henry had total clarity.

Thinking fast, not wasting the moment he was given, he did the only thing possible under the circumstances. He kicked backward with his right boot, right where he prayed the groin was for the man who was holding him.

As the sole of Henry's boot crushed something soft and yielding, the hands around his throat immediately let up and he dropped to the floor to gag and gasp, spitting bile as he sucked in a precious breath of air.

But he knew there was no time to spare and he looked up to see Abigail's husband, Philmore, bent over and wheezing from his crushed testicles.

Taking the initiative, Henry could see the large man was already recovering and there was no time to do anything but lunge at him. Henry hit Philmore low with his head down like a linebacker. Though Philmore was larger than Henry, the deadlands warrior was no small man either and the hit sent Philmore crashing back into an end table.

An oil lamp glowing softly sat on the end table, and when the large man hit it, the lamp fell to the floor, smashing and spreading burning oil in all directions. Some landed on Philmore and the man's clothing caught immediately, the material burning like dried newspaper, the stench of burning meat quickly filling the air.

But Philmore wasn't down yet, and though his hair had burned off and his face was melting, he roared in pain and anger and charged at Henry, who had stumbled backwards after hitting Philmore.

Reaching down, Henry pulled his panga from its sheath, the sixteen inches of steel, razor honed blade reflecting the flames like a mirror.

Henry waited for just the right time, and as Philmore came at him, Henry rolled to the side, came up in a crouch and jumped back at the flaming man, the panga raised over his head to come down in a chopping motion.

The panga found the back of Philmore's neck and cut more than halfway through before stopping. The weight of the dead man pulled the body forward and Henry held on to the hilt of the panga as the body slid off the blade to hit the floor with blood spurting out of the neck stump. Wherever the blood landed in the fire, the odor of burnt copper filtered into the air and Henry had to breathe through his mouth, not wanting to gag on the stench.

The flames were out of control now, the curtains and furniture catching and spreading to the walls, the old wallpaper adorning them excellent kindling for the growing inferno.

Stumbling through the room and back into the hallway, Henry saw Abigail on the floor, and Mary was underneath her. Dread filled him, as it looked like Abigail had killed Mary and was now dead on top of her. But then he saw Mary's hand wave to him and he rushed to the both bodies, grabbing Abigail and pulling her off Mary.

Coughing and wheezing, Mary rolled to her feet as she reached out and picked up her .38.

"Thanks, Henry, she almost had me, but I got lucky."

Henry glanced down at the corpse of the old woman to see the carving knife was embedded in Abigail's chest. It looked to Henry that the woman had attacked Mary but Mary had managed to grasp Abigail's arm and twist the knife back on her. When Abigail fell onto Mary, the knife slid into her chest easily, the old woman a victim of her own razor-sharp blade.

The room Philmore was in was now burning out of control. The fire had reached the bottles of alcohol sitting on top of the cabinet, more than half of the bottles having exploded from the heat, thus fueling the fire even more. The house was filling with smoke to the point Henry was coughing and hacking, as was Mary.

"We need to go, right now!" he yelled as a piece of the ceiling came crashing down, timbers burning like cordwood. He spotted his Glock on the hallway floor and he lunged for it, burning his palm in the process but not caring. The Glock was more than just a sidearm to him, he'd taken possession of it since the outbreak first began and it was a piece of his history, a part of his past life that he didn't want to forget. Back when he had first found the Glock, he was his old self, someone who was now long gone as he adapted to the new world of the living dead.

"Lead the way!" Mary replied as the two tried to reach the back door, which was closest.

But as they took their first few steps, they were blocked by licking flames, the fire flowing through the walls to now encapsulate all the rooms around them.

As the flames seemed to reach out at them with a life of its own, Henry backed away. "Head to the front door, we can't get out this way!" he yelled.

"No shit!" she replied, cursing in the heat of the moment, something Mary rarely did.

They backtracked through the house, but found the front door was closed off for them as well, the fire burning through the wall as if it was nothing more than tissue paper. It was easy to see that the old home was nothing but a giant tinder box just waiting for a match, one Henry had accidentally supplied.

Trapped in the hallway, there was nowhere to go and Mary huddled next to Henry, as he shielded her as best he could with his arms. His neck was raw from where Philmore had grabbed it and he was sure if he had a chance to look in a mirror, he would see that his neck would look as if he'd almost been hanged.

"What do we do?" Mary cried out as flames licked at her face.

"I don't know, give me a second!" he yelled back over the roaring fire.

"We don't have a second!" she yelled back as more of the ceiling in the next room collapsed, spewing soot and flames in all directions.

He knelt down with her so they could be closer to the floor, the smoke not as bad there but still not very good, and he knew he had seconds to figure a way out or they were both dead. He coughed some more, the smoke filling his lungs, sucking the oxygen from his body.

In his mind, the seconds ticked by unabated.

At the end of the driveway, Jimmy and the others stopped running, deciding they had gone far enough.

Cindy and Sue were standing together, and Raven was next to Jimmy, helping him stand.

"Where the hell are they?" Jimmy asked as he looked back at the house.

Raven took a step forward, pointing at one of the first floor windows. "There's a light there but it's not from a lamp or a flashlight."

Sue took a step forward. "Wait, I smell smoke."

"Yeah, so do I. Oh, shit, did someone start a fire in there?" Cindy asked as she moved up next to Sue.

Jimmy looked at each of them, already making up his mind. "We need to go back, they might be hurt," he said and pushed Raven away, standing on his own. He looked at Sue as he began to head back to the house, Cindy and Raven with him. "You stay here, Sue. Without a gun you'll just be another worry."

"Okay," Sue said, knowing she would be a liability.

"Come on, let's go," Jimmy yelled as he took off back down the driveway, towards the waiting house.

He didn't get more than halfway there before three windows on the first floor blew out, glass flying out to land in the snow. Immediately, flames licked out the windows, orange and red tongues reaching for the night sky. The roar of the fire could be heard as the inferno grew.

Jimmy stopped, staring at the flames, the fire reflected in the pupils of his wide eyes.

"Henry! Mary!" he screamed, gripping his shotgun tightly, knowing raw force wouldn't help this time. "We need to get in there, save them!" He was about to run at the house, ignoring the flames, when another explosion ripped through the house, sending him falling backwards. "Jesus Christ!"

Cindy and Raven were by his side, both helping him to stand. The lower half of the house was now a raging conflagration, parts of the siding burning as the intense heat inside burned through the inner to the outer walls.

Jimmy heard footsteps on the gravel, and he turned around to see Sue running to the house with eyes wide and her mouth open in a silent scream.

Jimmy ran to her, grabbing her and halting her forward movement. "No, Sue, it's too late!"

"Let me go, Jimmy, Henry's in there!" Sue yelled as she looked at the house. "Henry, where are you? Henry!"

Raven shook her head, her eyes watering slightly. "If they're still alive, they gotta be dead by now."

"No!" Sue screamed. "Henry! No, oh, God no!" She crumpled to the driveway, tears flowing down her face as Raven knelt down to console her.

Cindy went to Jimmy and he wrapped his arms around her. "Oh, shit, Cindy. Mary, Henry, it can't be. They were right behind us. This shouldn't be happening. Fuck, this can't be happening." He squeezed his empty hand into a fist, the other wrapped around the shotgun so tight his knuckles were bone white. "Fuck!" he screamed into the night, the loss of his two best friends overwhelming.

Cindy was sobbing softly at the thought that both Mary and Henry were dead, but as another explosion rocked the house, she knew the reality had to be faced.

"Goodbye, Mary," she whispered, praying her friend didn't suffer before the flames found her. "Bye, Henry."

From the back of the house, one of the windows was still intact, the massive inferno not yet reaching that part of the home with its fury. As the four companions either stood or kneeled in silence while watching the giant funeral pyre of their two fallen friends, the intact window suddenly exploded outward, glass raining down to land in the snow, twinkling like ice crystals. As the window exploded, a chair flew out to fall onto the ground, rolling three times before coming to a stop on its side.

All eyes went to the window, not understanding what was going on, and no sooner did the chair come to a stop, then something human-shaped, and burning, was thrown through the window to land in the snow. As fast as the shape landed, it began to move, to kick off the burning material of the rug it was wrapped in.

As the figure rolled away from the burning rug, all eyes went wide to see it was Mary.

"Holy shit, I don't fucking believe it!" Jimmy yelled as he ran at top speed to Mary, who was coughing and stumbling away from the house. She was in a daze, the smoke she'd inhaled causing her to falter as she tried to clear her vision.

Behind Jimmy, the others ran with him, each reaching Mary in seconds. Just as she was about to fall over, Jimmy was there to catch her.

"Jesus, Mary, you're alive!" Jimmy said as he caught her and cradled her like a baby. "Take it easy, you'll be fine. Are you hurt, are you burned?"

She shook her head, coughing as mucus rolled from her nose, down her lip and over her chin, her nose running from the smoke she'd inhaled. "I'm...okay...Henry...he wrapped me...tossed me out...where is he?"

"Shit, Henry's still alive?" Jimmy gasped before turning back to the house. "Oh, shit, where the fuck is he?"

The window that Mary had come through was brighter now, the flames finally attacking that part of the house, and Jimmy's hopes, just raised, were quickly dashed once more when he saw nothing inside the window but flames.

Sue and Cindy were with Mary now and they helped her walk away from the house, Jimmy standing with Raven as they stared at the window.

"Maybe he didn't get out in time?" she said. "Saved Mary, then the fire got him."

"I..." Jimmy began and then, from in the midst of the flames, Jimmy saw another shape come running at the window. As the figure jumped through the opening, Jimmy saw it was on fire, resembling a giant matchstick. The shape fell to the snow-covered ground and lay still.

"Raven, with me!" Jimmy ordered as the two darted at the form now lying still in the snow. The flames were crackling and hissing, and as Jimmy crossed the few feet, he saw it was another rug, something inside it once more. He had to hope it was Henry.

"Raven, put out the fires, hurry; use the damn snow!" Jimmy yelled and began to use his feet to kick snow onto the flaming carpet. Raven went to her knees and used her hands, and in seconds the fires were out, the carpet still smoking.

Jimmy dropped to his knees and went to pull the rug off whatever was inside, but he burned his left hand, the corner of the material still smoldering.

"Shit," he cursed as he scooped some snow and with the ice in his hand, he used it to pull back the rug, the hiss of melting snow carrying to his ears.

As he pulled back the rug, Jimmy saw the ash-gray hair that was so familiar to him, and with Raven helping him, he tugged on the rug some more, to expose a face covered with black soot, a pair of eyes looking up at him.

"Hey, buddy, how's it going?" Henry asked, his voice hoarse from smoke inhalation. No sooner did he speak then he coughed loudly, choking on mucus as he placed his forehead in the snow until the bout had passed.

"Jesus Christ, old man, don't fucking scare me like that," Jimmy said and helped Henry to his feet.

"Mary, is she...?" Henry began.

"She's fine, Henry, we got her, she's doing fine," Jimmy said.

Henry coughed some more, having to lean on Jimmy for support as he let the spasm fill his entire body, but eventually it passed. Jimmy and Raven helped Henry walk away from the house to get some clearance from it, and when Henry reached Sue, she ran into his arms, hugging and kissing him.

Cindy was with Mary, talking to her and both went to Henry, hugging him as Sue stayed glued to him. She wasn't about to let him go, not now, not after almost losing him.

Hocking a large ball of mucus, Henry spit into the snow. The mucus was black, more soot. He wondered if he'd be spitting up soot for the next week, his lungs were burning so much.

"Come on, let's get the hell out of here," Henry said as he began to walk down the gravel driveway, Sue helping him and carrying his full backpack, both he and Mary still carrying them when they jumped through the window.

The others followed, and by the time Henry reached the end of the driveway, he was walking by himself, his vitality and indomitable will taking over.

They didn't speak for the next fifteen minutes, each walking silently after the outpouring of emotion at the thought of losing two of their group, but when Henry, on point once more, crested a hill that overlooked the house, he stopped and leaned against a tree. The others gathered around him, each now gazing out to the burning house, a beacon of light in the middle of complete darkness.

Through the crackling of the flames, each of them heard the single scream.

No one was able to see where it came from, but as the fire touched the night sky, it seemed to come from the heart of the conflagration, gathering power and volume with each roar of the inferno. The scream rose higher and higher until it petered out, the last second of it filled with agony and despair.

And then it was gone, lost on the wind.

Each of the group looked at the other, wondering if what they had heard was real or just an effect of the fire.

"Maybe one of them was still alive," Mary surmised as she hugged herself, the scream still in her mind, haunting her despite the evil intentions of the owner.

"Doesn't matter," Henry said. "They're dead now and they got what they deserved. In the end, that's what counts." He turned and began walking away, in the direction of the road they had found previously. It had to lead somewhere and that would be their next destination. "Come on, people, we need to make camp for the night before we set out in the morning."

The others shifted their packs of food salvaged from the house and followed Henry, single file through the pitch black woods, while behind them, the house continued to burn, the inferno resembling a small piece of Hell that had found a home on Earth.

KNIGHT SYNDROME: TEMPLARS OF THE UNDEAD
by Jesus Morales

A young nun is commissioned to find the Pope's abducted daughter, but quickly realizes she is part of a bloodline of reincarnated saints, destined to fight against an evil relic that empowers creatures from beyond the grave.

Soon, she is thrown into a world she only dreamed of, filled with demons from her nightmares. With her very life hanging in the balance, she will battle the hordes of Hell, for if she fails, the consequences will be dire.

PLAYING GOD: A ZOMBIE NOVEL
by Jeffery Dye

It was supposed to be a regeneration virus to help soldiers on the battle-field—regrowing limbs and healing wounds— but a simple act of carelessness unleashed it on an unsuspecting world.

For the virus was not perfected, and once exposed, the host quickly dies, only to rise again as one of the undead.

As countries are quickly overrun, scientists and military teams battle to contain the outbreak.

There is no other option.

If the infection continues to spread, soon the entire globe will be consumed. And perhaps that will be a just punishment for a mankind that dared to try to play God.

DEAD HOUSE: A ZOMBIE GHOST STORY
by Keith Adam Luethke

The old mansion on the edge of town, aptly named Dead House, has a history of blood, pain, and death, but what Victor Leeds knows of this past only scratches the surface of the true horrors within.

But when his girlfriend is attacked by a shadowy figure one rainy night, he soon finds himself caught up in a world where the dead walk and ghostly wraiths abound. And to make matters worse, a pair of serial killers are fulfilling carefully made plans, and when they are done, the small town of Stormville, New York will run red. The last ingredient to open the gates of Hell, and plunge this small upstate town into madness, is rain.   And in Stormville, it pours by the gallons.

The Lazarus Culture
by Pasquale J. Morrone

Secret Service Agent Christopher Kearns had no idea what he was up against. Assigned on a temporary basis to the Center for Disease Control, he only knew that somehow it was connected to the lives of those the agency protected...namely, the President of the United States. If there were possible terrorist activities in the making, he could only guess it was at a red alert basis.

When Kearns meets and befriends Doctor Marlene Peterson of the Breezy Point Medical Center in Maryland, he soon finds that science fiction can indeed become a reality. In a solitary room walked a man with no vital signs: dead. The explanation he received came from Doctor Lee Fret, a man assigned to the case from the CDC. Something was attached to the brain stem. Something alive that was quickly spreading rapidly through Maryland and other states.

Kearns and his ragtag army of agents and medical personnel soon find themselves in a world of meaningless slaughter and mayhem. The armies of the walking dead were far more than mere zombies. Some began to change into whatever it was they ate. The government had found a way to reanimate the dead by implanting a parasite found on the tongue of the Red Snapper to the human brain. It looked good on paper, but it was a project straight from Hell.

The dead now walked, but it wasn't a mystery. It was The Lazarus Culture.

DEAD RAGE

by Anthony Giangregorio
Book 2 in the Rage virus series!

An unknown virus spreads across the globe, turning ordinary people into bloodthirsty, ravenous killers.

Only a small percentage of the population is immune and soon become prey to the infected.

Amongst the infected comes a man, stricken by the virus, yet still retaining his grasp on reality. His need to destroy the *normals* becomes an obsession and he raises an army of killers to seek out and kill all who aren't *changed* like himself. A few survivors gather together on the outskirts of Chicago and find themselves running for their lives as the specter of death looms over all.

The Dead Rage virus will find you, no matter where you hide.

CHRISTMAS IS DEAD: A ZOMBIE ANTHOLOGY

Edited by Anthony Giangregorio

Twas the night before Christmas and all through the house, not a creature was stirring, not even a. . . zombie?

That's right; this anthology explores what would happen at Christmas time if there was a full blown zombie outbreak. Reanimated turkeys, zombie Santas, and demon reindeers that turn people into flesh-eating ghouls are just some of the tales you will find in this merry undead book. So curl up under the Christmas tree with a cup of hot chocolate, and as the fireplace crackles with warmth, get ready to have your heart filled with holiday cheer. But of course, then it will be ripped from your heaving chest and fed upon by blood-thirsty elves with a craving for human flesh! For you see, Christmas is Dead!

And you will never look at the holiday season the same way again.

BLOOD RAGE

(The Prequel to DEAD RAGE)

by Anthony Giangregorio

The madness descended before anyone knew what was happening. Perfectly normal people suddenly became rage-fueled killers, tearing and slicing their way across the city. Within hours, Chicago was a battlefield, the dead strewn in the streets like trash.

Stacy, Chad and a few others are just a few of the immune, unaffected by the virus but not to the violence surrounding them. The *changed* are ravenous, sweeping across Chicago and perhaps the world, destroying any *normals* they come across. Fire, slaughter, and blood rule the land, and the few survivors are now an endangered species.

This is the story of the first days of the Dead Rage virus and the brave souls who struggle to live just one more day.

When the smoke clears, and the *changed* have maimed and killed all who stand in their way, only the strong will remain.

The rest will be left to rot in the sun.

THE BOOK OF CANNIBALS
Edited by Anthony Giangregorio

Human meat . . . the ultimate taboo.

Deep down, in the dark recesses of your mind, can you honestly say you never wondered how it might taste?

Honestly, never wondered if a chunk of thigh tasted like chicken or pork?

Or if a hunk of an arm was similar to steak? And what kind of wine would be served with it, red or white?

Would a human liver be no different than one from a cow, or a pig?

For all we know, human flesh is as tender as veal, better than the finest tenderloin. And that is what the stories in this book are about, eating each other. But be warned, after reading these tales of mastication, you may just become a vegetarian, or at the very least, think twice before taking your first bite of that juicy steak at your local restaurant.

DEADFREEZE
by Anthony Giangregorio
THIS IS WHAT HELL WOULD BE LIKE IF IT FROZE OVER!

When an experimental serum for hypothermia goes horribly wrong, a small research station in the middle of Antarctica becomes overrun with an army of the frozen dead.

Now a small group of survivors must battle the arctic weather and a horde of frozen zombies as they make their way across the frozen plains of Antarctica to a neighboring research station.

What they don't realize is that they are being hunted by an entity whose sole reason for existing is vengeance; and it will find them wherever they run.

VISIONS OF THE DEAD
A ZOMBIE STORY
by Anthony & Joseph Giangregorio

Jake Roberts felt like he was the luckiest man alive.

He had a great family, a beautiful girlfriend, who was soon to be his wife, and a job, that might not have been the best, but it paid the bills.

At least until the dead began to walk.

Now Jake is fighting to survive in a dead world while searching for his lost love, Melissa, knowing she's out there somewhere.

But the past isn't dead, and as he struggles for an uncertain future, the past threatens to consume him. With the present a constant battle between the living and the dead, Jake finds himself slipping in and out of the past, the visions of how it all happened haunting him. But Jake knows Melissa is out there somewhere and he'll find her or die trying.

In a world of the living dead, you can never escape your past.

DEAD MOURNING: A ZOMBIE HORROR STORY

by Anthony Giangregorio

Carl Jenkins was having a run of bad luck. Fresh out of jail, his probation tenuous, he'd lost every job he'd taken since being released. So now was his last chance, only one more job to prevent him from going back to prison. Assigned to work in a funeral home, he accidentally loses a shipment of embalming fluid. With nothing to lose, he substitutes it with a batch of chemicals from a nearby factory.

The results don't go as planned, though. While his screw-up goes unnoticed, his machinations revive the cadavers in the funeral home, unleashing an evil on the world that it has not seen before. Not wanting to become a snack for the rampaging dead, he flees the city, joining up with other survivors. An old, dilapidated zoo becomes their haven, while the dead wait outside the walls, hungry and patient.

But Carl is optimistic, after all, he's still alive, right? Perhaps his luck has changed and help will arrive to save them all?

Unfortunately, unknown to him and the other survivors, a serial killer has fallen into their group, trapped inside the zoo with them.

With the undead army clamoring outside the walls and a murderer within, it'll be a miracle if any of them live to see the next sunrise.

On second thought, maybe Carl would've been better off if he'd just gone back to jail.

ROAD KILL: A ZOMBIE TALE

by Anthony Giangregorio

In the summer of 2008, a rogue comet entered earth's orbit for 72 hours. During this time, a strange amber glow suffused the sky.

But something else happened; something in the comet's tail had an adverse affect on dead tissue and the result was the reanimation of every dead animal carcass on the planet.

A handful of survivors hole up in a diner in the backwoods of New Hampshire while the undead creatures of the night hunt for human prey.

There's a new blue plate special at DJ's Diner and Truck Stop, and it's you!

DEAD THINGS

by Anthony Giangregorio

Beneath the veil of reality we all know as truth, there is another world, one where creatures only seen in nightmares exist.

But what if these creatures do actually exist, and it is us that are only fleeting images, mere visions conjured up by some unknown being.

Werewolves, zombies, vampires, and other lost things that go bump in the night, inhabit the world of imagination and myth, but all will be found in this collection of tales.   But in this world, fiction becomes fact, and what lurks in the shadows is real. Beware the next time you sense you are being watched or catch movement in the corner of your eye, for though it may be nothing, it might just be your doom.

THE DARK

by Anthony Giangregorio
DARKNESS FALLS

The darkness came without warning.

First New York, then the rest of United States, and then the world became enveloped in a perpetual night without end.

With no sunlight, eventually the planet will wither and die, bringing on a new Ice Age. But that isn't problem for the human race, for humanity will be dead long before that happens.

There is something in the dark, creatures only seen in nightmares, and they are on the prowl. Evolution has changed and man is no longer the dominant species. When we are children, we're told not to fear the dark, that what we believe to exist in the shadows is false.

Unfortunately, that is no longer true.

SOULEATER

by Anthony Giangregorio

Twenty years ago, Jason Lawson witnessed the brutal death of his father by something only seen in nightmares, something so horrible he'd blocked it from his mind.

Now twenty years later the creature is back, this time for his son.

Jason won't let that happen.

He'll travel to the demon's world, struggling every second to rescue his son from its clutches.

But what he doesn't know is that the portal will only be open for a finite time and if he doesn't return with his son before it closes, then he'll be trapped in the demon's dimension forever.

SEE HOW IT ALL BEGAN IN THE NEW DOUBLE-SIZED 460 PAGE SPECIAL EDITION!

DEADWATER: EXPANDED EDITION

by Anthony Giangregorio

Through a series of tragic mishaps, a small town's water supply is contaminated with a deadly bacterium that transforms the town's population into flesh eating ghouls.

Without warning, Henry Watson finds himself thrown into a living hell where the living dead walk and want nothing more than to feed on the living.

Now Henry's trying to escape the undead town before he becomes the next victim.

With the military on one side, shooting civilians on sight, and a horde of bloodthirsty zombies on the other, Henry must try to battle his way to freedom.

With a small group of survivors, including a beautiful secretary and a wise-cracking janitor to aid him, the ragtag group will do their best to stay alive and escape the city codenamed: **Deadwater**.

DEAD END: A ZOMBIE NOVEL
by Anthony Giangregorio
THE DEAD WALK!

Newspapers everywhere proclaim the dead have returned to feast on the living!

A small group of survivors hole up in a cellar, afraid to brave the masses of animated corpses, but when food runs out, they have no choice but to venture out into a world gone mad.

What they will discover, however, is that the fall of civilization has brought out the worst in their fellow man.

Cannibals, psychotic preachers and rapists are just some of the atrocities they must face.

In a world turned upside down, it is life that has hit a Dead End.

BOOK OF THE DEAD 2: NOT DEAD YET
A ZOMBIE ANTHOLOGY
Edited by Anthony Giangregorio

Out of the ashes of death and decay, comes the second volume filled with the walking dead.

In this tomb, there are only slow, shambling monstrosities that were once human.

No one knows why the dead walk; only that they do, and that they are hungry for human flesh.

But these aren't your neighbors, your co-workers, or your family.
Now they are the living dead, and they will tear your throat out at a moment's notice.

So be warned as you delve into the pages of this book; the dead will find you, no matter where you hide.

LOVE IS DEAD: A ZOMBIE ANTHOLOGY
Edited by Anthony Giangregorio
THE DEATH OF LOVE

Valentine's Day is a day when young love is fulfilled.

Where hopeful young men bring candy and flowers to their sweethearts, in hopes of a kiss...or perhaps more. But not in this anthology.

For you see, LOVE IS DEAD, and in this tome, the dead walk, wanting to feed on those same hearts that once pumped in chests, bursting with love.

So toss aside that heart-shaped box of candy and throw away those red roses, you won't need them any longer. Instead, strap on a handgun, or pick up a shotgun and defend yourself from the ravenous undead.

Because in a world where the dead walk, even love isn't safe.

INSIDE THE PERIMETER: SCAVENGERS OF THE DEAD
by Alan Spencer

In the middle of nowhere, the vestiges of an abandoned town are surrounded by inescapably high concrete barriers, permitting no trespass or escape. The town is dormant of human life, but rampant with the living dead, who choose not to eat flesh, but to instead continue their survival by cruder means.

Boyd Broman, a detective arrested and falsely imprisoned, has been transferred into the secret town. He is given an ultimatum: recapture Hayden Grubaugh, the cannibal serial killer, who has been banished to the town, in exchange for his freedom.

During Boyd's search, he discovers why the psychotic cannibal must really be captured and the sinister secrets the dead town holds.

With no chance of escape, Broman finds himself trapped among the ravenous, violent dead.

With the cannibal feeding on the animated cadavers and the undead searching for Boyd, he must fulfill his end of the deal before the rotting corpses turn him into an unwilling organ donor. But Boyd wasn't told that no one gets out alive, that the town is a death sentence. For there is no escape from *Inside the Perimeter*.

DEADFALL
by Anthony Giangregorio

It's Halloween in the small suburban town of Wakefield, Mass.

While parents take their children trick or treating and others throw costume parties, a swarm of meteorites enter the earth's atmosphere and crash to earth.

Inside are small parasitic worms, no larger than maggots.

The worms quickly infect the corpses at a local cemetery and so begins the rise of the undead.

The walking dead soon get the upper hand, with no one believing the truth.

That the dead now walk.

Will a small group of survivors live through the zombie apocalypse?

Or will they, too, succumb to the Deadfall.

THE DEAD OF SPACE: BRAVE NEW WORLD
by Jeremiah Coe
Welcome to the future of the walking dead!

The Earth is freezing over. After a deep space probe returns with information of another habitable planet at the end of our galaxy, a desperate attempt to save mankind is implemented. The Intrepid, a massive starship with a crew of 500, is sent to investigate the world designated E-eleven-two for possible habitation of the human race. The world looks perfect, clear springs, tall mountains, open fields, even the remnants of the planet's native inhabitants still exist, right down to the structures they one lived in. And there are no native species to threaten the newly arrived human population. It's perfect...it's paradise. A mystery arrives in the form of the planet's previous inhabitant's corpses, found frozen under the polar ice caps, thousands of them, all perfectly preserved. The scientists, in their excitement, hastily bring back fifty of the bodies to base camp, each one perfectly preserved and ready to be dissected and studied. As the bodies thaw out and await dissection, first one, then another begins to move, and soon, they start to walk; despite being dead for hundreds if not thousands of years. The crew of the Intrepid are about to find out what happened to the natives of E-eleven-two, and are going to discover to their horror that they didn't die out naturally. In fact, there was nothing natural about their demise.

The future isn't full of hope...the future is dead.

ETERNAL NIGHT: A VAMPIRE ANTHOLOGY
Edited by Anthony Giangregorio

Blood, fangs, darkness and terror...these are the calling cards of the vampire mythos.

Inside this tome are stories that embrace vampire history but seek to introduce a new literary spin on this longstanding fictional monster. Follow a dark journey through cigarette-smoking creatures hunted by rogue angels, vampires that feed off of thoughts instead of blood, immortals presenting the fantastic in a local rock band, to a legendary monster on the far reaches of town.

Forget what you know about vampires; this anthology will destroy historical mythos and embrace incredible new twists on this celebrated, fictional character.

Welcome to a world of the undead, welcome to the world of Eternal Night.

BOOK OF THE DEAD
A ZOMBIE ANTHOLOGY VOL 1
ISBN 978-1-935458-25-8
Edited by Anthony Giangregorio

This is the most faithful, truest zombie anthology ever written, and we invite you along for the ride. Every single story in this book is filled with slack-jawed, eyes glazed, slow moving, shambling zombies set in a world where the dead have risen and only want to eat the flesh of the living. In these pages, the rules are sacrosanct. There is no deviation from what a zombie should be or how they came about. The Dead Walk.

There is no reason, though rumors and suppositions fill the radio and television stations. But the only thing that is fact is that the walking dead are here and they will not go away. So prepare yourself for the ultimate homage to the master of zombie legend. And remember... Aim for the head!

REVOLUTION OF THE DEAD
by Anthony Giangregorio
THE DEAD SHALL RISE AGAIN!

Five years ago, a deadly plague wiped out 97% of the world's population, America suffering tragically. Bodies were everywhere, far too many to bury or burn. But then, through a miracle of medical science, a way is found to reanimate the dead.

With the manpower of the United States depleted, and the remaining survivors not wanting to give up their internet and fast food restaurants, the undead are conscripted as slave labor.

Now they cut the grass, pick up the trash, and walk the dogs of the surviving humans.

But whether alive or dead, no race wants to be controlled, and sooner or later the dead will fight back, wanting the freedom they enjoyed in life.

The revolution has begun!

And when it's over, the dead will rule the land, and the remaining humans will become the slaves...or worse.

KINGDOM OF THE DEAD
by Anthony Giangregorio
THE DEAD HAVE RISEN!

In the dead city of Pittsburgh, two small enclaves struggle to survive, eking out an existence of hand to mouth.

But instead of working together, both groups battle for the last remaining fuel and supplies of a city filled with the living dead.

Six months after the initial outbreak, a lone helicopter arrives bearing two more survivors and a newborn baby. One enclave welcomes them, while the other schemes to steal their helicopter and escape the decaying city.

With no police, fire, or social services existing, the two will battle for dominance in the steel city of the walking dead. But when the dust settles, the question is: will the remaining humans be the winners, or the losers?

When the dead walk, the line between Heaven and Hell is so twisted and bent there is no line at all.

RISE OF THE DEAD
by Anthony Giangregorio
DEATH IS ONLY THE BEGINNING!

In less than forty-eight hours, more than half the globe was infected.
In another forty-eight, the rest would be enveloped.
The reason?

A science experiment gone horribly wrong which enabled the dead to walk, their flesh rotting on their bones even as they seek human prey.

Jeremy was an ordinary nineteen year old slacker. He partied too much and had done poorly in high school. After a night of drinking and drugs, he awoke to find the world a very different place from the one he'd left the night before.

The dead were walking and feeding on the living, and as Jeremy stepped out into a world gone mad, the dead spotting him alone and unarmed in the middle of the street, he had to wonder if he would live long enough to see his twentieth birthday.

THE CHRONICLES OF JACK PRIMUS
BOOK ONE
by Michael D. Griffiths

Beneath the world of normalcy we all live in lies another world, one where supernatural beings exist.

These creatures of the night hunt us; want to feed on our very souls, though only a few know of their existence.

One such man is Jack Primus, who accidentally pierces the veil between this world and the next. With no other choice if he wants to live, he finds himself on the run, hunted by beings called the Xemmoni, an ancient race that sees humans as nothing but cattle. They want his soul, to feed on his very essence, and they will kill all who stand in their way. But if they thought Jack would just lie down and accept his fate, they were sorely mistaken. He didn't ask for this battle, but he knew he would fight them with everything at his disposal, for to lose is a fate worse than death.

He would win this war, and he would take down anyone who got in his way.

THE WAR AGAINST THEM: A ZOMBIE NOVEL
by Jose Alfredo Vazquez

Mankind wasn't prepared for the onslaught.

An ancient organism is reanimating the dead bodies of its victims, creating worldwide chaos and panic as the disease spreads to every corner of the globe. As governments struggle to contain the disease, courageous individuals across the planet learn what it truly means to make choices as they struggle to survive.

Geopolitics meet technology in a race to save mankind from the worst threat it has ever faced. Doctors, military and soldiers from all walks of life battle to find a cure. For the dead walk, and if not stopped, they will wipe out all life on Earth. Humanity is fighting a war they cannot win, for who can overcome Death itself? Man versus the walking dead with the winner ruling the planet. Welcome to *The War Against Them.*

END OF DAYS: AN APOCALYPTIC ANTHOLOGY
VOLUMES 1 -4
Edited by Anthony Giangregorio

Our world is a fragile place.

Meteors, famine, floods, nuclear war, solar flares, and hundreds of other calamities can plunge our small blue planet into turmoil in an instant.

What would you do if tomorrow the sun went super nova or the world was swallowed by water, submerging the world into the cold darkness of the ocean? This anthology explores some of those scenarios and plunges you into total annihilation.

But remember, it's only a book, and tomorrow will come as it always does. Or will it?

ANOTHER EXCITING CHAPTER IN THE DEADWATER SERIES!
DEADRAIN
by Anthony Giangregorio

Welcome to the New America, population: 0

When a bacterial outbreak contaminates America's lower atmosphere, the resulting rain mutates into a deadly conduit for death.

Human's all over America are exposed and within a matter of days society has crumbled and the walking dead rule the land.

The America we know is gone, replaced by a new order; where the dead walk and humans are the prey.

Henry Watson and his small group of companions travel the country, searching for someplace better, someplace where the rain is safe.

In the New America the rules have changed; survive or perish.

THE BOOK OF CANNIBALS

ISBN 13: 978-1-935458-52-4   ISBN 10: 1-935458-52-3

ARE YOU HUNGRY YET?

Blood of the Dead
A.P. Fuchs

Bits of the Dead
edited by
Keith Gouveia

Axiom-man
The Dead Land
A.P. Fuchs

Wicked East Press
Publisher of Fine Fiction Anthologies

coming soon...

www.wickedeastpress.com